ADVANCE PRAISE FOR

Three Rooms, Shared Bath

Three Rooms, Shared Bath—what an intriguing title. This is a delightful book, following a widow who decides to rent out three bedrooms in her large house on eastern Long Island. She has interesting renters, some of whom stay for months. And, of course, she has those who are a pain in the neck. Some become life-long friends, and, as goes with the territory, some she needs to kick out sooner rather than later. You get a flavor of the Hamptons in the summer season. But the real joys in the book are the interactions between the landlady and her guests. I enthusiastically recommend this book.

—James R. Callan, author, Father Frank Mystery Series

* * *

"With humor and candor, Eileen Obser reflects on the ups and downs, and many surprises, of renting rooms to people of all ages, backgrounds, and personalities. Landlords and tenants will get a kick out of it!

—Debbie Tuma, Hamptons journalist, TV and radio host

* * *

"Start this delightful tale with the map, noting Shinnecock Indian Reservation. If you live in the Hamptons, you'll love this book."

—Elizabeth Robertson Laytin, East Hampton author and playwright

Three Rooms, Shared Bath

A Landlady in the Hamptons

Eileen Obser

an imprint of Sunbury Press, Inc.
Mechanicsburg, PA USA

an imprint of Sunbury Press, Inc.
Mechanicsburg, PA USA

FIRST BROWN POSEY PRESS EDITION: July 2021

Set in Adobe Garamond | Interior design by Crystal Devine | Cover Art by Ashley Shumaker | Cover by Lawrence Knorr | Map by Jeffrey Obser | Edited by Abigail Hensen.

Publisher's Cataloging-in-Publication Data
Names: Obser, Eileen, author.
Title: Three rooms, shared bath : a landlady in the Hamptons / Eileen Obser.
Description: First trade paperback edition. | Mechanicsburg, PA : Brown Posey Press, 2021.
Summary: *Three Rooms, Shared Bath* is the story of Diana Long, a middle-aged widow, who rents rooms in her East Hampton home because she needs the income.
Identifiers: ISBN : 978-1-62006-507-5 (softcover).
Subjects: FICTION / Small Town & Rural | FICTION / Women | FICTION / Literary.

Product of the United States of America
0 1 1 2 3 5 8 13 21 34 55

Continue the Enlightenment!

For my children, Suzanne and Jeffrey

Author's Note

Three Rooms, Shared Bath, is a work of fiction. Characters and incidents are products of the author's imagination.

The year is 2008, and the tourist season this Labor Day week is winding down in the Hamptons. Summer tenants are leaving, other tenants are moving in for the off-season, and landlords and landladies can only hope their new guests will adhere to the house rules.

Hampton celebrities, locales, places of interest, summer events, shops, roads, restaurants, and landmarks are real, as are details of the 2008 Democratic National Convention and other news stories of the week.

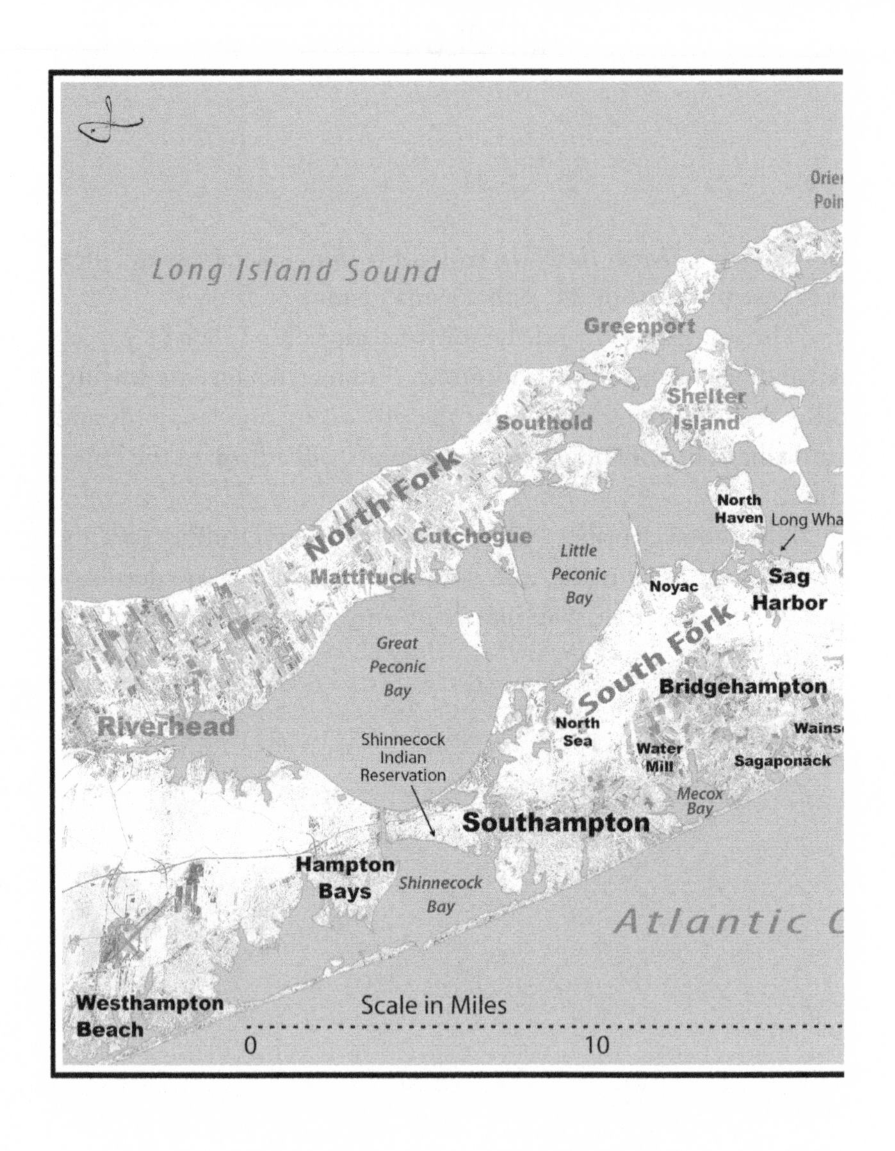
Long Island Sound
Greenport
Shelter Island
Southold
North Fork
Cutchogue
Mattituck
North Haven
Little Peconic Bay
Noyac
Sag Harbor
South Fork
Great Peconic Bay
Bridgehampton
Riverhead
North Sea
Water Mill
Sagaponack
Shinnecock Indian Reservation
Mecox Bay
Southampton
Hampton Bays
Shinnecock Bay
Westhampton Beach
Scale in Miles
0
10

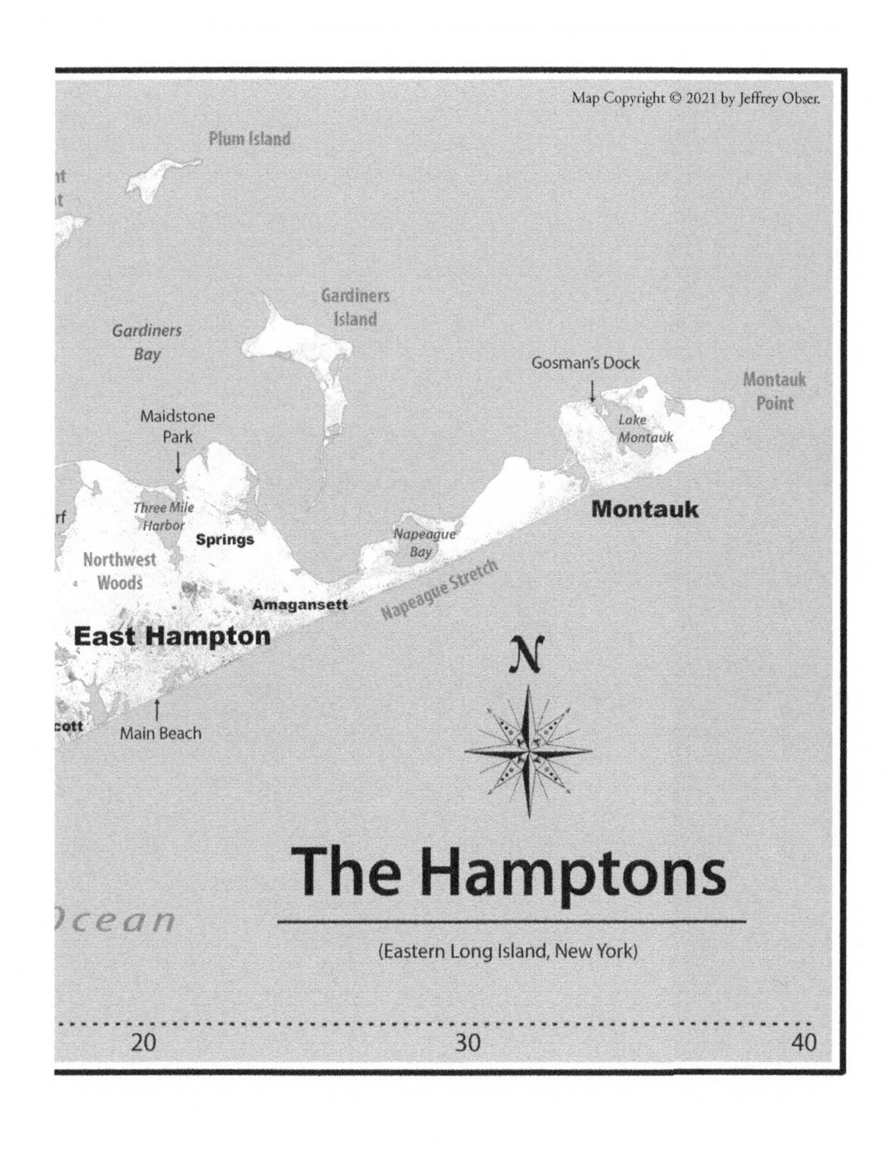
Map Copyright © 2021 by Jeffrey Obser.
Plum Island
Gardiners Island
Gardiners Bay
Gosman's Dock
Montauk Point
Lake Montauk
Maidstone Park
Three Mile Harbor
Springs
Napeague Bay
Montauk
Northwest Woods
Napeague Stretch
Amagansett
East Hampton
N
Main Beach
The Hamptons
(Eastern Long Island, New York)
20
30
40

RULES FOR TENANTS:

No smoking or drugs or weapons in house.

Chapter One

The call came after lunch on Wednesday afternoon.

"*Allo.* My name is Basia," the woman said. "I see in the newspaper that you have room?"

It wasn't a Spanish accent. As an ESL teacher, Diana spotted those easily. There were so many Latinos living in the Hamptons—from Mexico, Columbia, Ecuador, and other countries.

"Yes." Diana held the phone to her ear as she cleared the table and rinsed her plate and cup. "I have a room. Do you need it in September?"

"No. I need room right now."

"Now? Right before the Labor Day weekend?"

"I am looking for place year-round," Basia said. "I am living in house two years now. It is too much. They smoke. They drink. They using drugs. They crazy. And I am getting crazy, too!"

"Where are you from?" Diana managed to ask. She straightened the pile of *New Yorkers* and other magazines and books on the hall shelf as she spoke, then turned off the TV. Enough news for now about the Democratic convention. Later, she would tune in again.

"Poland. I am Polish. Basia Godlewski. But I am here 14 years. I am citizen."

Amazing; so many years in the U.S., and she still hadn't lost that thick accent. Diana wondered about her vocabulary skills. But no, she wasn't asking her to teach her better English; she just wanted to find a room.

"Do you have a job out here, Basia?" A standard question, as in: can you afford the rent?

"Yes. I am massage therapist at spa in Sag Harbor. "I no trouble. I don't drink or smoke. I am very clean and quiet."

They all said this, more or less. "I'm quiet." "I'm clean." "I can pay the rent on time." After the tenants moved in, a different story began to unfold. In their minds, they probably were clean, quiet, and cooperative.

Perhaps it's my brain that's at fault. Diana checked her eye makeup in the hall mirror. She couldn't see things the way most of these tenants did. And, to be honest, she didn't want strangers living in her house anymore. Since Gary died, she depended on the income.

"You can come over and see the room," she told Basia. "I have a smaller one also that I can show you. After this weekend, the larger room I advertised will be available."

"I come at six o'clock today, after my last massage appointment, okay, Missus—what is your name?"

"Diana Watson. That will be fine. I look forward to meeting you." She gave her the directions. "See you soon."

Wally, her big black Lab, started barking, so she let him out the back door and smiled at her two cats, Cassie and Juan, curled up on the living room sofa. Then she turned up the music she had been playing earlier. Every day, as she cooked or did chores around the house, she loved exercising to different kinds of music.

"You like it too, don't you?" she said, stroking the cats. They were sister and brother, short-haired, gold and white in color. "This is party time for you."

Diana wore a short white skirt and a tight blue T-shirt over her "generous chest," as a girlfriend of hers called it. Later, she would take off her sneakers to stretch her feet and toes. Brushing back her hair, still naturally blond in middle age, she began to dance.

Smiling and humming, she started moving up and down, slowly doing her arm, shoulder, and leg stretches, followed by a series of squats and bridges on the carpeted floor. She then went into a graceful, gliding, improvised dance across the living room, oblivious to everything but the music and her dancing.

The music from *West Side Story* resonated throughout the empty house.

> "I like to be in America,
> okay by me in America. . . ."

She sang along with Rita Moreno as she hip-hopped and mamboed, her arms wide open, embracing the air, the world.

There was a quote by Cicero hanging from the wall over her desk:

> "It is exercise alone that supports the
> spirits, and keeps the mind in vigor."

Yes, let it be so, Diana thought, executing a backbend while moving her arms and hands up and down in waves.

As she rose from the floor—her arms, legs, and torso still in full motion—she noticed that George, the lawn guy, was in the back yard, staring in the window, smiling. Or was it *leering*? Tall, broad, and bushy-haired, he had said he would come over and trim the lawn and shrubs before the holiday weekend. It was a lovely day; sunny, around 74 degrees with low humidity and no wind.

Stopping mid-step, she waved and smiled back. The central air was on, so the doors and windows were closed.

Thank God I'm not dancing around in a bra and underpants.

Bad enough, George had to observe her generous chest and "muffin" middle. She imagined him talking about her, "this lady I work for in town," at Wolfie's Tavern or Bucket's Deli, to other locals, or Bonackers as they were known. These landscapers, plumbers, contractors, and fishermen's heritages, in some cases, went back centuries. Many of the original Bonac families in Springs, north of East Hampton village, were among the town's earliest settlers, having come from England, possibly Kent, Dorchester, or Dorset.

"She looked pretty good, I must admit," George might say, in his noticeable Bonac dialect, hoisting a brew and smiling.

"Wouldn't mind if my old lady could dance around the room like that. Yes, yes, bub!"

The cats ran to hide, and Wally barked as the huge lawn mower started up. "Damn!" Diana took the record off the turntable, clicked off the stereo, and opened the sliding door to the deck. "Come on in, boy," she called. "You can play again later." She hugged him around the neck and gestured to the stereo. "Me, too."

While changing into a long skirt and loose T-shirt, she turned on the TV for another short while. The theme for the day in Denver was "Securing America's Future." Joe Biden, the Vice Presidential candidate, would be speaking, as would Bill Clinton.

She checked the small upstairs room to make sure it was neat and presentable before Basia arrived. The bathroom was grungy, which it tended to get with male tenants like Mark. The toilet was filthy, and the seat was up. Whisker hairs were in the sink, and the tub had a wide green ring around the sides.

The cleaning woman came once a month, which was as much as Diana felt she could afford. Her next visit was on Wednesday, right after Labor Day. Grabbing the bottle of cleanser, she whisked some into the sink, the tub, and the toilet before proceeding to clean everything. Then she picked two damp, grayish-white towels off the floor and put them in Mark's closet. She hid his dirty brush and comb, his slimy, rusting razor and shaving cream under the sink.

Brett, her other summer tenant, usually kept the bathroom cleaner, but he had been busy at work and had hardly been at home the past week.

Mark, who rented the largest bedroom, right above her dining room, was young, tall, and pleasant looking, with dark, wavy hair and a slight beard. Just out of college, he had arrived in mid-June as a summer renter, but "Hey," he told her, "I may decide to stay here year-round." He was caddying at a local golf club. They discussed her general rules of the house. He didn't smoke, "but I used to experiment," he told her with a slight grin, "with different substances." And, he added, he would only drink while living here "off the premises."

The room had been Diana's master bedroom. After Gary died, she moved downstairs to the large room that had once been their office before becoming his sickroom. It was now her bedroom and office combined, big enough for her queen-sized bed, dressers, and bookshelves, plus her spacious office area—desk, computer and printer, file cabinets. The large skylight above her desk gave her much pleasure in all seasons of the year. Besides the trees, she loved watching the moon passing over and the stars, plus the lightning, rain, and snowstorms.

Mark came in with an attitude and would leave with one. On his second Saturday living in the house, he asked Diana for directions to Hampton Bays. He and his friend, Colin, a short, quiet fellow who had moved in when Mark did, into the third and smallest bedroom upstairs but who left in mid-August, were going to party there, he told her.

"I hear that's *the* place for drinking and hot babes." He pointed to his friend. "Colin here is a real chick magnet."

"I suggest you don't drive home, Mark," Diana said. The police were everywhere on summer weekends looking out for young men like him. "If you plan on drinking with the hot babes, you'd better sleep in your car or at someone's house or behind a dune on the beach."

But Mark didn't take her advice. Colin came home alone in the middle of the night, via a $125 taxi ride from Hampton Bays, a distance of twenty miles; Mark had been locked up overnight for driving while intoxicated.

"Why didn't you guys listen to me?" she asked Colin.

He shrugged his shoulders, climbing slowly and straight-faced up the stairs to his room.

George finished mowing the lawn and was walking down the driveway to his truck. Diana had left his money, fifty dollars for a basic cut and weed-whacking, in the mailbox. She looked closely at the green areas in the front and back of the house, a white, two-story saltbox on a wooded acre of land, with a footpath leading to the street. There were many trees—all oaks mostly, with sassafras, beech, and pitch pines—so there wasn't much lawn to be mowed. Much of the groundcover was moss and weeds, and George did a great job keeping the place tidy.

Diana did the planting, which she enjoyed; a variety of colorful annuals filled the planters and garden beds and hanging baskets. And she added new perennials and deciduous plants each year, ordering them from local nurseries and through the mail. She had learned a lot from Gary over the years, especially after he left his CPA firm and took up landscaping full time.

Sometimes she went with him on jobs, planting alongside him and helping him decide what might be added to his clients' landscapes—hydrangeas here, rhododendrons there. Butterfly bushes in that corner; Japanese andromeda in this one. Gary listened to her advice with an open mind and encouraged her to take gardening classes. She did so with the Cornell Cooperative Extension and became a Master Gardener.

"But I don't want to work with you full-time," Diana told him. "I have other things I'd rather do."

Gary had secured his landscaping license and his liability insurance. "Okay," he said, "so you'll help sometimes, and you'll continue being my muse?"

"Correct."

"Good arrangement, sweetheart," he said, hugging her and then laughing. "Let's go check the boxwoods. See what they think."

As a volunteer at the Horticultural Alliance of the Hamptons for the past five years, Diana kept the large library organized, helped with the mail and the monthly newsletter. She was also able to advise visitors and callers on most gardening matters:

"Should I use topsoil or gardening soil?"

"Compost this area or not?"

"What won't the deer eat?"

Those were some of the easier questions the staff was able to answer. And if none of them on board could explain, there was always someone out in the field who could and would.

The frequent programs HAH sponsored—garden tours upstate and elsewhere, film screenings and discussions—kept providing her with more useful information to keep and to share.

"Getting to Know the Native Plants," a recent roundtable discussion and "Reconsidering your Cutting Garden" were two events she had helped coordinate in the spring; coming up in the fall was a whole new schedule.

She was glad that Gary enjoyed his last years. His job grew boring; he was a Senior Manager at his company by the time he left, commuting in and out of Manhattan from their home in Kew Gardens, Queens. While the kids were growing up, and until they both were in college, he stayed with it. Thankfully, that house was paid for, and the East Hampton house, where they spent more and more time, had low mortgage payments.

Diana returned to school to get her Master's in Library Science; night classes. She then worked as a librarian and, in time, paid off her college debt. They were grateful; there were no debts, just the usual month-to-month expenses.

"I love my new vocation," Gary told everyone. He advertised and kept finding new landscaping clients, sometimes by referrals. He even hired a helper in his last year, a young man who learned so much and quickly, just as Diana had.

Right before the pains started, and he was diagnosed with cancer, Gary bought a large commercial mower and a pick-up truck. Pancreatic cancer, they were told, was seldom detected in its early stages, only when it was too late. No hope in hell he would pull through, although the doctors didn't quite put it that way.

In one long container on the rear deck, Diana had her herbs—basil, parsley, oregano, rosemary. She had painted the planter bright yellow and green and stuck a wooden lady chef on a stick in the middle. Sniffing the air, she smiled at the beauty and simplicity of it all.

When thoughts of downsizing—selling the house, moving away, and changing her life came up—and, lately, they did more and more, she looked around and thought, *How could I ever let this go?*

Wally wagged his tail at her side as she worked. "We're going to grow old here together, right, baby?"

He was Gary's surprise gift one year before he died, to himself more than to her "I've always wanted a black Lab, honey," he said, presenting the small, furry, black puppy, all face and ears and tail. And from that time on, she was Wally's mom, whether or not she wanted to be.

With the children raised and gone, Diana had felt they should travel more, that they should do more exploring of places and things away from the Hamptons. They shouldn't have to find a pet sitter or board a dog at the kennel every time they wanted to take off for new adventures.

Wally, all 80 pounds of him, sat with her now in the quiet backyard as she stared up at the clear blue, late August sky. He was only a dog, but he allowed her to pet him and whisper sweet nothings in his ear. Now he licked her hand and face and cradled his long face in her lap. When Diana wanted to fill up the huge hole created by loss and loneliness, Wally seemed to sense it. He was always nearby.

"I guess I'm a very lucky mom to have you," she said now. He wagged his tail and looked up lovingly at her with his big, dark eyes. "C'mon," she whispered, kissing his head. "Let's go inside. I have work to do."

Chapter Two

Diana checked the computer, but there was nothing that needed her immediate attention. During this last summer week, the local news was concerned with the crowds of tourists and happenings in the villages, plus events coming up in September, on the East End, and in the city.

Nationally, the whole country was riveted to the news because of Barack Obama's nomination for president. Last night, on the second day of the convention, Diana sat alone in the living room and watched as Hillary Clinton spoke to a rousing audience of what seemed like thousands of Democrats. To cheers and clapping, Clinton said how happy she was to be there and how pleased she was to be a "proud supporter of Barack Obama." The beaming faces of Bill Clinton, Joe Biden, Michelle Obama, and other Democrats shone on the screen. About halfway through her speech, Hillary said, to more applause and cheers, "I support Barack Obama for President. 'No way. No how. No McCain.'"

Besides the convention, there were the usual celebrity doings, sports results, and stories of crimes and misdemeanors. A traffic accident; two people were killed. A man murdered his wife, then committed suicide.

The crimes part reminded her of Monday, two nights ago, when she told her friend, Frank, about Mark's arrest in early June.

He sighed. "I've been telling you since Gary died: sell the goddamn house and invest the money; then you won't have to deal with all those weirdo tenants."

His white hair and mustache glowed under the track lights along the high ceiling. She thought of him as a good-looking guy, with his wide smile and broad forehead, but now, with his large brown eyes and pursed mouth, he seemed like some kind of loopy wizard. All he needed were a top hat and a wand. Diana hated when he got into a bossy mode.

They were eating dinner, their weekly night out. Their system was: he paid one week, she paid the next. Cittanuova, one of the popular restaurants in the village, was packed since it was late August, the last big weekend in the Hamptons. Frank had ordered the chicken parmigiana and Diana, the whole baked fish, served with fennel potato crisps, lemon-oregano conserva, and olive oil.

"Daurade royal," the waiter said earlier when she questioned what kind of *pesce* they used. He smiled when she used the Italian word. "Imported from Europe," he said.

"*Il pesce è delizioso.*"

"Oh, God, yes." Diana bit into the firm, tasty flesh of the fish. "I feel like I'm in Italy. Venice or Florence, maybe."

"Yes." Frank was digging happily into his chicken entree. "*Mangia, Signora*!"

They raised their wine glasses. "To the good life," Diana said.

"I'll drink to that," Frank replied. "You invest the money from the sale of the house, get a nice check each month, and go live in a small cottage or condo somewhere. End of story. And . . ." he raised a finger in the air, "the beginning of a much happier life."

Diana's knife crashed to the floor as she pushed back from the table. "Damn it, Frank Ross, you're my dear friend, but how many times do we have to go over this?"

Frank gestured for the waiter to bring another knife. "C'mon, relax now. *Buon apetito*!" He reached across the table and kissed her hand. "You're so beautiful when you get angry. That long blonde hair, those flashing green eyes. . . ."

Diana pulled back her hand. "Why should I leave? I don't care if the house is worth a lot of money. I can manage without selling it. Gary invested well, so I have money, even if it's not a fortune. I teach. I have some savings. I *do* manage."

Frank sighed. "Right, Mrs. Watson. On your peaceful acre in the Northwest woods." He glared at her. "Except it ain't peaceful, not with those idiots who move in and out and make you nuts. You tell me the stories, and you make *me* nuts."

My own damned fault, Diana thought. She shouldn't have told him about that former tenant, Mary, and how she propped Diana's brand new TV on a rickety cardboard carton, and it crashed to the floor. Or how she was always late with the rent. She had also complained about Mark. Not suitable for conversation during dinner.

She continued eating. "I have so many ties in this area, Frank: good friends, my students, my work at the Horticultural Alliance and at Guild Hall. You know this. My kids know this." She tried to keep her voice low in the bustling restaurant. "After all this time, I still love living out here."

"Ah, yes, the beautiful Hamptons, where it's still possible to live amid God's bountiful nature without too many neighbors or too many McMansions taking over the farmlands or, heaven forbid, the street you live on."

"Are you writing a story, or are you listening to me?"

"Me write a story? *You* should write the story, sweetheart. 'How I Keep from Drowning in an Ocean of Debt While Fishing for Decent Tenants.'"

Frank leaned over the side of the small table and pretended to be pulling in a big fish. The well-dressed, Spanish-speaking foursome eating in the nearby booth looked at him like he might be drunk or *loco*.

Diana rolled her eyes. "Very funny. You're the journalist. Put that in one of your articles. It hasn't been bad this summer. One really good tenant. . . ."

"And one whack job," Frank sighed. "And his whack job buddy."

The waiter took away their plates and handed them the dessert menu. "We have a special tonight. *Torta di Cioccolato*. It is a flourless chocolate cake with a hazelnut center, panna gelato, and chocolate sauce."

"Yum." Diana smiled. "I'll have gelato, please. One scoop of rum raisin." They made the gelato in-house, and she loved it.

"Coffee, please," Frank said. "I've had more than enough." He indicated that his belly was full.

After dinner, they strolled through the village. It was cloudy and humid. The temperature was in the mid-60s. Main Street was jammed with "slicks," as Frank referred to them: "slick clothing, slick cars, slick houses, and slick attitudes."

"Don't lose me." Diana held on to his arm. Besides the pedestrians, there were dogs of different sizes and baby strollers to contend with, plus Starbucks containers and dripping ice cream cones. Frank and she looked at each other as they noticed a tall, suntanned, executive-type guy in a yellow plaid shirt, navy shorts, and Sperry topsiders. He was smoking a cigar.

"Okay," Frank said in a low voice, "is that a Republican or a Democrat?"

"I wonder where he parked the yacht." Diana looked around.

A woman and child passed by, wearing identical Ralph Lauren straw hats with paisley trim. "We should get those and wear them when we walk through town," Frank said. "We'd look adorable."

Diana laughed. "You see the shopping bags?" All around them were logos for Coach, Gucci, Elie Tahari, Calypso. And Ralph Lauren, of course. The village had become so ridiculously upscale since she moved here years ago with Gary. "You'd never know the country is having a financial crisis, right?"

Frank nodded. "The Great Recession. Yeah, a rough time for lots of folks." He looked to his right and left. "You wouldn't know it; not out here." Then he smiled. "Good thing we don't have the dog with us."

Diana loved to walk Wally through the village. The tourists, and especially the children, asked to be introduced and to pet him. When the sidewalks were this crowded, she usually walked him away from Main Street, down Newtown Lane, or alongside Town Pond, on the way to the ocean at Main Beach. They turned right on Lily Pond Lane sometimes and strolled past Martha Stewart's estate, with its properly maintained flowers blooming on the lawn outside the hedgerows. Wally would often pee or poop there, and then she would walk with him down to Georgica Beach, near Stephen Spielberg's property.

Frank and she attended Authors Night in early August, an annual benefit for the East Hampton Library. More than 80 writers were signed up for the event, held under a huge tent at the library grounds. Alec Baldwin, the honorary co-chair, greeted people in attendance, including Diana and Frank, with a handshake and a "Hi, there."

Robert Caro, author of the Lyndon Johnson biographies and *The Power Broker*, was there, along with Jay McInerney, E. L. Doctorow, Dava Sobel, and Tom Clavin, all well-established writers who lived locally. Dan Rattiner, the founder and editor of *Dan's Papers*, was there with his newest book, *In the Hamptons: My Fifty Years with Farmers, Fishermen, Artists, Billionaires and Celebrities.* Diana bought the book, and Dan autographed it.

As a journalist, Frank knew many of the authors and introduced her to some of them, including Michael Schnayerson, who wrote for *Vanity Fair* and whose latest book, *Coal River,* was on display.

At the huge buffet table, Diana had a pleasant conversation with Philip Shultz, who had just won the Pulitzer Prize for *Failure,* his newest collection of poems. She had met him before, at a Guild Hall reading. "Oh yes, I remember you," he said to her, bowing slightly and smiling.

By 7:30, people were leaving, returning to their cars with their new books, while over 20 of the writers would go on to private parties hosted by local residents.

"You know how much I care about you," Frank said as they drove back to her house. "I'm not the only one concerned about your welfare. I'll bet your kids would agree that you should move on. Gary, God rest his soul, would say yes, too."

"Move on means move *out*, Frank. Move out of the state, maybe into the hidden hills of Kentucky or the coal mines of West Virginia." She sighed. "I'll get online to FindYourSpot.com again, okay? Just to make you happy. Maybe they've come up with new locations since I last checked: Bali Ha'i, Glocca Morra, Oz."

"Wise-ass." Frank leaned over to kiss her cheek. "Don't go off to one of those places, okay? I won't be able to reach you by cell phone."

"Oh, I'd never want to be out of touch with *you*, Frank. I'd have nobody to tell me what to do with my life."

"Sweet dreams." He blew Diana a kiss as she got out of the car and waved him off.

It was still light enough, so she walked around all sides of the house, checking the flowers that were in bloom; the geraniums and impatiens and marigolds. The hibiscus were gorgeous, all pink and white and purple. Gary had planted those shrubs the first year they moved in.

Wally was watching her through the rear slider, and he barked to be let out of the house. Diana climbed up to the wooden deck and unlocked the door. He jumped out and was all over her, his tail wagging, his tongue licking her hands.

"Well, hi there, big boy, did you miss me?" She hugged him. "Do you want to move away with Mama, like Daddy Frank thinks we should do? Where should we go?"

Mosquitoes attacked suddenly, right at her arms and face. She swatted at them with her hands. "Phooey! Someplace where they don't have bugs. Let's go inside."

"Maybe you should have kept running the place as a B&B," Frank had said at the restaurant after she told him about Mark's arrest. "People are in and out only on weekends. You'd have the middle of the week to yourself."

"I got tired of the turnover," Diana told him. "Those faces and names were a blur after a while. I was a laundress and a cleaning lady. I hated all the housework. And I had to keep putting out continental breakfasts: fruits and breads, cakes and jams, coffee and tea, juices."

"You put the stuff out on the kitchen counter. They helped themselves."

"True, but I had the guests in my face—in the kitchen, in the dining room. I'd look out back, and they were sitting on the deck. They wanted to talk; I kept praying they'd go off to the beach. Go anywhere."

"You *let* them do that. You could have told them to stay in their rooms. Eat in the driveway or in their cars."

"You'd make a lousy B&B manager, Frank."

"True," he said. "But you were good at it. You told me you enjoyed it."

"I figured this might be easier. Same people all summer, right through fall. Off-season tenants now and then." She sighed. "But it's sure hard to deal with ones like this kid, Mark."

"You could go back to being a librarian. I know you stopped because Gary got sick, but you could still get a job doing that. Part-time, since you don't want full-time."

"I think about that. I enjoyed the work, but I prefer part-time teaching now. And my volunteer work."

He shook his head. "You don't want to listen to any of my ideas. You won't let me help you."

"You can help me by passing that bread basket," she told him, smiling.

RULES FOR TENANTS:

Minimum alcohol, please.

Chapter Three

Frank, a freelance journalist and photographer, was separated from his wife, and he had become friends with Diana and Gary soon after they moved to East Hampton full time. The three of them had long conversations about life, literature, and current events. Some evenings they went to the movies together or played Scrabble. They discussed Frank's book-in-progress about his family, from their history in Scotland to life in the U.S. Frank spoke about it; Gary and she listened. Occasionally, they were able to add a useful idea for his research.

After Gary was diagnosed with cancer, Frank sat with him for hours and drove him to the doctor for tests. He took him down to the ocean, making sure he was bundled up in a jacket and towels when they sat on beach chairs to look out at the waves. They talked about gardening, although that wasn't Frank's favorite subject, and he read books aloud from the gardening shelf in the hallway.

"This one's a doozy," he said one day, holding up a well-worn volume. "Is this your favorite book? *Pruning Simplified*? Now, this is something special to curl up with on a quiet winter night. I would be asleep in two minutes."

They all laughed, and Gary autographed the book and bequeathed it to Frank. "Make sure you add this to my will," he told Diana.

When he was dying, the children, Jennifer and Dennis, flew in to be at his side. Frank was there, too, just like a member of the family. At the funeral, he gave the eulogy:

"This was a good man, my close friend, and I'll miss him. My heart goes out to Diana and to his children. They know how much their father loved them." He gestured toward the casket. "This is a man who was a successful businessman and who changed careers later in life. He loved his work. How many people can say that? Gary loved being a landscaper, working the earth, being with the earth."

Frank paused then and looked around at the crowd. "Now, my friend, you are truly part of the earth. God bless."

He lived in a small cottage about a mile away, and though he teased Diana and flirted with her, she didn't consider it a romance.

"You're a beauty," Frank told her on a rainy afternoon in July. They were drinking tea in her kitchen. "I'd love to wake up in the mornings and find you in bed next to me or in the kitchen making my breakfast."

"Dream on, my love." Diana gazed up at the ceiling.

He picked up a pen and pretended to write on the table. "She was the fairest of the fair, with a dancer's body and grace. Light, clear skin, blonde curls framing her soft green eyes and a mouth that begged to be kissed. . . ."

"Nice compliments," she said with a laugh, "but lousy writing."

He tore the sheet from her pad and handed it to her.

"Thanks," she told him. "I'll save it with my vast collection of love letters."

Now, on this Wednesday before Labor Day weekend, Diana remembered that July conversation with Frank. He was a wonderful guy in many ways—sincere, funny, and genuine—but the chemistry was never there. Not for her and, deep down, she didn't believe it was there for Frank either.

She still thought about Kenneth, the one special man in her life since Gary died. They met while she was traveling to Seattle to visit Dennis. He sat next to her on the plane. Tall and thin, with blond hair and tan skin, his horn-rimmed glasses made him look scholarly. He wore a gray suit and a red and blue striped tie, which he loosened, then removed, during the flight. On his lap, propped on his leather briefcase, was *A Short History of the World* by J. M. Roberts, a thick paperback he was halfway through reading.

"Looks interesting," Diana couldn't resist saying. One, because she knew about the book, as a librarian. Two, because he had to be an intelligent person, reading it.

"Very small print, you'll notice," he said, turning toward her. "And over 500 pages. I have to wear these glasses." He took them off and held them at a distance. "Only for reading but, to be honest, I do a lot of reading."

Diana smiled. "I do too."

An hours' long conversation followed—books, the economy, food, jobs, travel. His left arm often nudged hers, unintentionally, from his aisle seat across to hers, at the window. They were pleasant bumps, or alerts, as if to say, "Here I am; pay attention."

There were dates, phone calls, and emails. There was lovemaking. He came to New York to see her. She traveled to see him.

They talked about living together, but he wanted it to be on the west coast. He was a professor in the MBA program at the University of Washington. Gary had an MBA from Columbia University. It was one of the first things Diana told Kenneth. He had a BS in Economics, too, as did Kenneth. Both men were close to her heart, and they had the same educational backgrounds. Also—an odd coincidence—they were both left-handed.

In her desk drawer, she found her small journal and packet of photos tucked in its sides. Love souvenirs. She had written down Kay Knudsen's quote:

> "Love is missing someone whenever you're apart,
> but somehow feeling warm inside because you're
> close in heart."

While visiting Dennis, she took the ferry to Bainbridge Island, where Kenneth lived. She didn't tell her son about her possible new man, not right away. Gary had died only one year earlier. And what was Kenneth doing now? After ten months, they decided not to keep in touch. By mutual agreement. How hard was that, though?

Not to pick up the phone or the pen; to be tough and maintain silence, dignity, and self-respect?

If ever she was tempted to sell the house and move away, it was then. But she couldn't do it. The relationship ended. *Too far away*, she told herself. *Too goddamned far away*. She felt tears now and reached for a tissue.

Diana thought of telling Frank about Kenneth but never did. He probably would bring the affair up again and again, perhaps out of jealousy, teasing her, taunting her, maybe without realizing it. She didn't want the memory pressing down on her mind, like an ongoing unhappy ending in a movie.

She ran down the hall to open the door for Wally. "In and out. In and out. I'm not only a landlady," she said, letting him pass by while the two cats ran outside. "I'm a *door lady*."

The house seemed in good order. She had fluffed the pillows, dusted the furniture, even sponge-mopped the kitchen floor. Basia should be here soon. She grabbed the upright vacuum and went over the rugs in the halls, upstairs and down. Lots of pet hair accumulated in this house, thanks to Wally and the two cats.

She had allowed Brett, the other tenant, in bedroom number two, the medium-sized room, to bring his dog along for the summer. Only twenty years old, Brett had one more year to finish college and was interning with a well-known local architect.

They spoke many times by phone before he arrived in mid-May, and Diana enjoyed the conversations; he was a student at the University of Chicago and would attend graduate school in architecture next year

"Oh, you'll love it out here," Diana told him. "This is Charles Gwathmey country, Richard Meier, Norman Jaffe, Frank Gehry. . . ."

"Yeah, I know," Brett said. "I've only seen pictures. I'm looking forward to seeing their work out in the Hamptons."

They talked about his family, who lived in Delaware, where Diana also had relatives. She told him about her children, and her teaching of English as a Second Language.

Brett had told Diana that Buster was a small dog, but, actually, he was a good-sized mutt, a "Schnoodle" she would find out, a cross between a Miniature Schnauzer and a Poodle. Two-tone brown, he had curly, fuzzy fur and a sweet face.

"You lied." Diana was surprised when they first appeared at the door. "This is not a tiny dog."

"To me, he is. He's only thirty pounds." Brett seemed sincerely contrite about her disappointment. "Be small!" he commanded Buster. "We don't want to get thrown out on the street by this nice lady. We'll be homeless."

A pleasant-looking young guy, of medium height, with bushy eyebrows and a full head of light brown hair, Brett scooped the dog up into his arms. "See?" He moved closer to Diana. "Small. Please, nice lady," he said, holding up Buster's paw and speaking in a high voice, "oh, *puh-leez* don't put us out in the street. I'm quiet, I don't shed, and I get along with everyone. Even cats and dogs. You'll love me!"

"Okay. Enough already." Diana laughed. "I hope you don't plan on becoming a mime or a puppeteer, Brett."

"Not unless I fail at all my other jobs." He patted Buster on the head. "Good boy."

No extra dog would have been best for a household that already contained one large dog and two cats. But they hit it off, Brett and Diana, and, as promised, he took the dog to his office each day, to the architectural firm where he was working.

She went with him to visit Gates of the Grove, the impressive sanctuary of the Jewish Center of the Hamptons, designed by Norman Jaffe. They also drove to Amagansett to see the Robert Gwathmey house on Bluff Road that their son, Charles, had designed. Since his parents' death, Charles used this as his weekend residence.

"He was only 27 years old when he designed that," he told Diane.

The summer was only beginning, and Brett had already impressed her and his bosses with his intelligence and talent. He was gay, which Diana had figured out early on, and seemed to be a well-adjusted, self-satisfied soul.

Sometimes they took their dogs for walks in the evenings, down to Main Beach, or through the village. Occasionally, they had dinner or dessert together outside at Babette's Restaurant on Newtown Lane, the dogs resting nearby. Diana knew the owner for years, and she would join them at their table when she wasn't busy.

"Mark just called me," Diana told Brett back in June. It was noon on Sunday, the day after Mark's arrest. "He asked if I'd drive to Hampton Bays to bring him home from jail."

"That nervy bastard," Brett said. He was at his office. "You should throw him out."

When Mark first arrived to stay, Diana asked if he had a good trip from Michigan.

"I got a speeding ticket on the way here," he told her, "right on the Long Island Expressway." This, she knew, probably didn't help his case later on, when he was arrested in Hampton Bays. He was smiling as he spoke, bragging actually, while he preened in the kitchen, shirtless and wearing short-shorts.

Mark had run the dishwasher, even though it held only a few dirty dishes. He had four huge glass beer mugs in the machine. "Souvenirs," he said proudly. "I was the fastest drinker at the bar. I wanna display these upstairs on the shelf."

"I'm very proud of you, Mark." Diana gave her best attempt at a smile. She had a quick, unpleasant vision of him sitting upstairs, four frosty mugs of beer in front of him, and downing them one after another. "Please let me run the dishwasher when I feel it's time."

"Yes, *ma'am.*" Mark's large mouth flattened in sarcasm. He took his four mugs and swaggered out of the room. She wanted to smack him; throw a frying pan at him; order him to leave her home that instant.

"See you later, *ma'am,*" Mark called from the stairwell.

Chapter Four

A bright yellow Volkswagen Beetle convertible raced up the driveway. The top was down on this cool, dry early evening. Diana watched as a tall blonde woman got out and walked toward the house. *Basia.*

She was at the front door as Diana opened it, and Basia quickly engulfed her in a warm, tight hug. Like they were lifelong friends, family even, her Polish relative from the old country.

Basia was taller than Diana, in her mid-thirties, with blue eyes and bright red lipstick. She was well-tanned, and waves of streaked blond hair fell about her face, kind of movie star-ish, Diana thought. She wore a white T-shirt that spelled "Diva" in green and silver sequins and white gym pants. And she smelled of citrus, fresh and pleasant.

"I am so happy to meet you," Basia said, giving Diana another hug. She looked around the hallway. "What a lovely house. I will be so happy here." She spied Wally, who was wagging his tail, trying to get close to her.

"You are such a wonderful doggie." She bent down to hug him and planted a big kiss on his head. "I help take care of you. Momma will be so happy I watch after you." Wally rolled over on his back. "I rub you, yes, I give you good exercise." She reached up and handed Diana a burr that the dog probably picked up in the bushes. Was he about to get a massage, Diana wondered? "You be my pet, too. Is that okay, Mr. Wally dog?"

"Let me show you around."

Diana wondered about the gregariousness of this young woman; it seemed a bit phony. In her experience, men made better tenants. She nearly always had trouble with women. For one thing, fragrances would fill the air, most of which Diana disliked and was allergic to—perfume, soaps, lotions, detergents. Late-night telephone calls and boyfriends sleeping in were other problems, and she, the house mother/landlord, always had to put a stop to it. Or try.

"Here's the kitchen." She led Basia through the rooms. "Do you cook a lot?"

The young woman was smiling, with Wally close by her side. "I love to cook but am so busy with my schedule that I have not much time." She smiled. "My boyfriend, he cooks for me sometimes. He very good cook."

A boyfriend. She had mentioned this on the phone. And Diana did say that the room was for one person only. "Your boyfriend, Basia, do you stay at his house?"

"Oh, yes. But other people are in his house, so not too often."

"I can't have other people, guests, sleeping over, Basia." She led her upstairs to show her the two rooms. "My ad in the paper clearly states one person only." She spoke softly. "I know it's a problem for my tenants who are in relationships."

Basia pouted. "Well, he *is* my boyfriend, after all. But I understand you must have rules."

Yes, Diana said to herself, a *whole list of them.* Which this gal might or might not obey. The boyfriend might be here one night a week or five.

Whenever Frank reminded her that this tenant business was a lot of work, she knew that he was right. Of course, it was work. But some of the tenants remained friends long after they were gone. Diana received holiday cards and emails, keeping her up to date on their lives. Some had been part-time tenants while starting up businesses, such as the owners of Babette's, or people building houses in East Hampton. And many of them, like Brett, were excellent company.

"This is the room that's available right now," Diana told Basia, leading her into room number three. "As I told you, it's small."

There was a single bed, two small dressers, a desk, and a chair, plus a closet.

When they first moved into the house, this was the third bedroom. The original owners had their builder bring water pipes up into the closet. Gary loved that; he thought he might create a darkroom in there and take classes in photography, although he never followed through with that idea.

The ceiling was sloped, as was the entire front roof of the house. One window let in the light. Diana furnished the small room with a pale green carpet, white see-through curtains, and a multi-striped bedspread. A framed Monet print was on one wall; a large film poster for *Casablanca* in shades of light brown was on the other. People who stayed here over the years, whether for months at a time or just for weekends, called the room "charming" and "cozy." Bed and breakfast guests used to request it especially. She had a matching second twin bed, stored in the basement right now, which was used as needed for couples.

"Yes," Basia said with a frown, "is small. Is okay for short while, but I have so many things."

"I'll show you the larger room."

And when Diana opened the door to Mark's room, across the hall, Basia practically shouted. "Oh yes, this is wonderful room. This is so perfect for me!"

The room was spacious, with three windows, and overlooked the driveway, the yard, and the gardens. It was bright and cool, made cooler with the central air Diana ran all summer. Colorful matted and framed prints hung on the white walls, one of birch trees in winter, another of St. Mary's Lake in Glacier National Park, in Montana, surrounded by mountain ranges, with puffy white clouds reflected in the lake on a sunny day. Gary and she had camped there for several days one summer. Set diagonally across from the TV stand were a white wicker rocking chair and side table. The bright blue wall-to-wall carpeting added to the room's charm.

"Please ignore that." Diana pointed to a huge pile of Mark's laundry near the closet and on the rocker. "He's not the neatest tenant, I'm afraid."

"It is fantastic, this room."

Basia then ran out of the room to see the bathroom. Her enthusiasm was contagious. Diana started to laugh.

"Compared to where I am," Basia said, "this is Waldorf-Astoria. This is the Plaza."

"It's a shared bath, as you must know, with the other two rooms." Diana joined her by the bathroom door. "It's a full bath, you see, bathtub and all."

"I think it will be fine," Basia said. "I am used to sharing bath. No problem."

As they walked back down the stairs, Diana said, "I'll need a reference or two. Do you have references?"

She could hear Frank's voice echoing from the walls: "Don't you check the backgrounds of these people? You could get a serial killer in there. Next thing you know, I'll be going to your funeral."

"Yes." Basia nodded. "I give you my boss's number. He will tell you I'm very good worker."

"No," Diana said, "I'm sure you *are* a good worker, but I need to have a personal reference."

Basia was petting Wally again, down on all fours with him. "You are the cutest doggie. Yes, you are."

Diana watched this, wondering if this woman would really be helpful and let the dog out when she expected to be home late. Many tenants offered to do this when they moved in, but when Diana called them and asked if they could do it, they usually had to "work late" or were "going out right from work," or "won't be home until tomorrow."

"I go home and pack and move in tomorrow. That's okay?" Basia got to her feet. "I will sleep in little room."

"Oh, it's fine." Diana shrugged. "About the references . . ."

"Yes, yes, here's my boss's name and number." She grabbed the notepad and pen Diana kept on the kitchen counter and wrote the information down. "I cannot give you landlord as reference. I never see her; she never comes to the house. Robert, the one in charge, he won't want to hear about reference. I don't tell him I am leaving."

"Okay," Diana wished she was at the beach suddenly, listening to the sounds of the ocean surf instead of having this conversation. "I'll call your boss. Is she there now?"

"Perhaps."

Basia fumbled in her purse to find her wallet. "I give you two hundred dollars deposit. That's okay?" She handed Diana two one hundred dollar bills.

"As I told you on the phone, Basia, I have to have to have first and last month's rent, plus security."

"I give Robert the rent only two days ago." She frowned. "Was stupid. Now I don't have so much money." Her face brightened. "I get paid on Friday; I give you more then."

Diana looked at her directly. "Please tell me honestly: will you be able to pay me the rent, now and each month, on time?"

"Yes, yes, of course," Basia replied, avoiding Diana's stare.

She didn't have to be hit on the head to recognize some duplicity in this Polish beauty's soul.

"I move in tomorrow at my lunchtime, maybe one o'clock. This is okay?"

No, Diana's smart voice said. "Yes," is what her dumb voice replied.

Maybe it would be all right. Maybe this blond cutie would surprise her and be an outstanding tenant. She could only hope. Get rid of Mark; have Basia here instead. *Would it work*?

Basia left, throwing her a kiss. "I go home and start packing right now. Maybe I leave there tonight and stay at my boyfriend's. I am so happy." She flashed a smile, jumped into her yellow convertible, and took off, her hair flying, and was gone.

Diana wanted to call Frank and tell him about the interview, but she didn't want to hear him rant about her handling of it. In July, when Mark was annoying her by microwaving garlicky Texas Toast almost every night, then leaving smelly dishes in the sink for her to clean up, she complained to Frank.

"Look," he said, "I'll get a divorce. Marry me, for Christ's sake! Then you won't have to bring in any more of these god-awful tenants."

"Just like that? You'll pay my bills? I can be worry-free about money for the rest of my life? Are you that wealthy?"

He sighed and gritted his teeth. "You know that I care about you. I'm sure you would be a wonderful wife. What are we waiting for?"

Diana leaned over and kissed his cheek. "You remind me of an old grizzly bear, Frank. That's not the way you propose to a woman."

"What do you want from me?"

"You're my friend, Frank. How many times do you have to bring this up? I want to remain your friend. Always."

He practically growled. "Don't keep complaining to me about these people. I can't solve your problems because you won't *let* me help solve them."

Now, in the silent kitchen, Diana remembered Frank's words. He meant them, and she knew he really cared for her, but she still couldn't see how he could solve all her problems by marrying her.

"I had my marriage," Diana told him. "Once was enough for this lifetime."

"So we've got to wait until the next lifetime?" Frank sighed but soon laughed. "We may come back as giraffes. Or bats. What then?

On the calendar, she noticed that Teresa, her ESL student from Mexico, would be here tomorrow, Thursday morning. Tam, the young bride from Vietnam, was coming the following day, Friday. She gathered the materials she would need for Teresa's class and sat down at the dining room table. They met here each week; it was where Diana held most of her classes. As a private ESL tutor by choice, she liked to work with adults who had at least finished high school. Sometimes she went to students' homes or met them at the library, in a private room, but she preferred teaching here, where it was quiet, with all her books and notes nearby. The central A/C made it extra pleasant in summer; she didn't even have to leave the house.

She grabbed *Mastering American English* and *The Ins and Outs of Prepositions* from the bookshelf. Spanish-speaking students were especially bad with prepositions.

With her folder of assignments and Teresa's special folder in hand, she sat down to plan a class. The phone rang, but Diana didn't recognize the number on her caller ID, so she ignored it. The person didn't leave a message. *Wait,* she thought. *What if that's a well-paying weekend guest for the small room*? She thought of calling back, but no, it was too late. Basia had paid; even if it wasn't enough money, she was moving in.

From the stereo came the soft melody of Percy Faith and his orchestra: "Theme from A Summer Place." Standing up, Diana danced around the living room a few times, doing arm and neck stretches—it felt so good and removed some of the tension, the "*Basian* tension." She did some slow turns and knee bends before going back to the table to prepare for tomorrow's meeting with Teresa.

Now she turned on the TV. On Monday night, she had watched Michelle Obama give her speech at the Democratic convention in Denver. She spoke to the theme of "One Nation" and said, movingly, that her husband didn't care where you were from or what your background was. The audience was quiet as she continued, saying that he knew the thread that connected us—our mutual belief in our country's promise and our dedication to our children's future—was strong enough to hold all Americans together as a nation even when some people disagreed.

Diana's eyes glistened as she listened to Michelle's gentle but powerful words. *What a lovely, gracious woman*, she thought.

Senator Ted Kennedy also spoke. Diane would find out later that he reduced his talk to 10 minutes, about half the length he intended. It was only his second time in public since he underwent surgery for a brain tumor. Kennedy spoke about hope—new hope for the many, not just for the few.

The beaming faces and cheers in the audience continued, and it was the same when Hillary gave her much longer speech on Tuesday night. Diana had listened to every word. There was no barrier too great or a ceiling too high for those who worked hard, Hillary said, summing up by entreating Democrats to elect Obama and Biden for "a future worthy of our great country."

More cheers, clapping, everyone standing up, and this went on and on.

An Independent, Diana was going to vote for Obama. All this ceremony being carried out was gratifying. It would be a new kind of government, and the country would be better for it. She thought of calling Frank to share her thoughts; he was probably watching, too. He was more political than she was, but both agreed that the Democrats were the best choice this year.

She put Percy Faith back on the stereo, hoping the gentle melody would calm her down so she could read *The New Yorker* for a while, then relax in bed with a book before going to sleep.

RULES FOR TENANTS

Room is for one person only;
No overnight guests.

Chapter Five

Tonight, Wednesday, the theme at the convention was "Securing America's Future." Vice-President Joe Biden spoke, followed by former President Bill Clinton. Another night of TV and speeches. Frank called before and again after the speeches. "You watching, Diana?"

"I sure am."

"Amazing how they scheduled all this, one day after the Beijing Olympics and a day before the Republicans set down in Minnesota. And with a hurricane out there. What a busy time in the news."

"I know that you followed the Olympics, Frank. We spoke about that on Monday."

"Right. We won the highest number of medals this year. And that swimmer, Michael Phelps impresses the hell out of me. Eight gold medals this time."

"Bill Clinton's going to speak. I've got to go."

"Yeah, me too. *Ciao.*"

And then the former president was onstage. He looked delighted and said that although his candidate didn't win, he was proud of the campaign she ran. She would do everything she could now to elect Obama. And amid all the applause, he said, "that makes two of us." Plus the rest of the country, of course. More applause. He spoke for 25 minutes.

Diana remembered her "Clinton moment" a few years ago, well after his presidency, when he was visiting in the Hamptons, with Hillary, for some fundraising event.

As she stood on the corner of Cedar Street and North Main Street, near the firehouse, waiting to walk across, a caravan of black limos drove down to the traffic light. Diana knew it was Clinton's entourage. Residents knew he'd be in town; it was in the local news.

But which car was his? She would find out as, suddenly, a rear window of one of the cars lowered, Clinton's face appeared, and he waved to her.

She waved back, stunned somewhat, but pleased. It was a memorable moment.

Biden was speaking then. Handsome as usual, Diane thought. He said that Barack touched and inspired people; he watched him do this all the time. Then he spoke about change and how and what we—Obama and the new presidency—would do for the country.

After speaking for about 20 minutes, he was joined on stage by his wife, Jill.

Mrs. Biden looked happy as she waved to the audience, and she alluded to a special guest about to arrive.

Barack Obama walked into view at that moment, and the crowd exploded.

Now it was Thursday, a lovely, cool morning. The rear door to the deck was open.

"Hello, Diana, are you in there?"

The front door opened, and Teresa walked inside.

"Yes, dear. Come on in." She was dressed but still putting on her eye makeup. Never a morning person, Diana often had to be up and out or ready for students she met here because of her ESL teaching. Before that, it was because of her job as a librarian. It was 9:30 right now; she would work with her student for the next hour and a half, at least.

"How long has it been that you have been teaching me?" Teresa asked once they were seated at the table. Diana served hot tea and a plate of small cinnamon crullers.

"It's been almost six months." She read over her notes in the folder. "Are you feeling more confident these days? Speaking with the school staff?"

"I think so. Maybe . . . sometimes more than others."

Teresa, her thin body neatly framed in a summery blue and green dress, had pinned her long, curly black hair at the sides, and she wore thick, brown-rimmed eyeglasses. In her late forties, she never married and had once wanted to be a nun. She came to the States from Mexico with a Master's degree in Education and, until this year, worked as a housekeeper, the way so many immigrants did. She was here on a temporary visa, teaching Spanish as of last September to sixth-graders at a private school. An American friend had recommended her to the principal and, by luck, Teresa showed up at exactly the right time and got the job.

Diana never asked if her ESL students were legal or not. The more educated they were, the more open they were about their immigration status. But she didn't judge them. There were others in the community and the media who did this. If her students asked for advice, she gave it. If they needed letters written to the immigration authorities, she helped with that, too.

"Did you have your pre-fall term interview with the vice-principal?"

"Ah yes, Mrs. Fortunato. The bitch!"

Diana laughed. "Your English has really improved so much. Did you call her that? And did she throw you out of the room?"

Teresa smiled. "She didn't look at me but said, 'Ms. Valdez' . . . just like that, '*Ms.* Valdez' . . . her nose up in the air like all the time."

Diana interrupted, "Like *it was* all the time. Add the noun and the verb."

"Right. She says to me, 'Do you enjoy working here at our school?' As if she is owner of the whole building." She frowned.

"And I say, 'Oh, very much, Ms. Fortunato.' I cannot bring myself to call her by her first name. The others, they call her Emily. I can't do this. This is why I need help, as I tell you always. I must stop being afraid that I don't lose my job. They all speak English so beautiful, so perfect—"

Diana interrupted again. "Beautiful*ly*. Perfect*ly*. Correct use of adverbs."

Teresa sighed. "*Aye yai yai*!"

"I've told you so many times," Diana said softly, "nobody speaks English flawlessly. Even the best-educated, English-speaking Americans make mistakes in conversation and writing."

"Thank you, darling." Teresa grabbed Diana's hand. "You always make me feel better."

"Have you ever read Mark Twain?"

"Oh, yes. I know *Huckleberry Finn*."

"There's a quote by him you should know. Let me see." Diana paused to get it right:

> "I have traveled more than anyone else, and I notice
> that even the angels speak English with an accent."

"That is wonderful! Write it down for me, please. I want to share it with my family."

"I'll do that but, meanwhile, let me see your writing assignment."

Their tutoring sessions usually went like this. Some conversation, some reading and grammar practice, and a review of a student's writing.

As she pulled out the two sheets of paper, Teresa held them up and smiled. "'Waiting,' you said as the subject. You know, I think I use this idea for my students this fall. One-word assignments. It's very good."

Diana raised her hand. "I think I *will* use this. Or, I think I *am going to* use this. Complete sentences, teacher lady!"

Teresa groaned and made the sign of the cross. "I'm worse than the children, dear Jesus."

"No. You just talk faster than you think. We've discussed that many times. Slow down."

"You see why I'm afraid of Emily . . ." Teresa winced. "I try to talk slow, but how can she respect me if I miss some words?"

"That's part of your accent. You're obviously an educated woman, a dedicated teacher, and it's perfectly okay to leave out a word here and there with Ms. Emily."

The telephone rang, and Diana got up from her chair.

"Excuse me, Teresa, I have to get that."

She nodded and leaned over to read over her work.

"Hello, Basia, what's up?"

"It may be 12 o'clock noon that I come by. Is that okay with you? You are at home?"

"Yes, I'll be here," Diana told her. "Thanks for letting me know."

She went back to the table. "A new tenant, I think. Do you want more tea?"

"No, darling, this is fine. So you have someone new coming to stay here?"

"Yes. She wants to move in right away."

Teresa reached out to touch her hand. "I hope she's a good person."

"Me too."

During their sessions, she had spoken about various tenants, complaining about some, praising others. And Teresa had met a few, reserving her comments unless asked her opinion, "He seems like a good person," she might say. Or, "Is it okay for you to have that man in your house?"

"Here is my writing."

Diana took the neatly typed pages in her hand. She was glad Teresa had come now for her lesson before Basia started moving in. She tried to keep people from dropping by, telephoning, or interfering in any way when she was working with her students.

"Waiting," she read. Diana held her printed copy, pen in hand for editing. "You enjoyed writing on this topic?"

She nodded. "Many, many thoughts came to me. So many things to wait for in life; so much time and effort." She gestured. "Well, you read."

Teresa wrote about waiting for her mother to be released from the hospital, back in Guanajuato, where she was born and raised. Her mother had suffered a stroke, and the family had decided "Mama" should return to her home and that her daughter would leave the *convento* where she was a *noviciado* to take care of her. Teresa had neatly typed the English translations of the Spanish terms in parentheses.

> "I was worried about my mother, and I loved her so much, but I did not know how I would feel leaving the convent. I prayed hard and waited to have word from God that it was okay. I could leave that place and do His will by taking care of my mother."

"This is beautiful writing," Diana said.

"*Gracias,*" Teresa replied. "I mean, 'Thank you.'"

Diana looked up from the paper. Teresa knew the rule very well: No Spanish spoken here, only English was allowed.

The essay continued:

> "My family and me waited . . ." Diana crossed out "me" and put in "I" . . . "for the time when the doctors would say it was time for Mama to leave the hospital. It was weeks. My mother had relapses . . ."

"Relapses?" Diana stopped reading at this. "Do you mean your mother had more strokes?"

"Yes. *Si.* We say in Spanish, '*sufir una recaida.*' They were small, but the doctors, they had to watch her carefully."

"This is so touching," Diana said. "And cut out the Spanish!"

Teresa giggled. "Okay, teacher."

Diana read the next part out loud:

> "For me, it was not only that I would be leaving the convent to take care of my mother. I knew that if I left, I would not be coming back. For many months, before Mama became sick, I was thinking: is this truly what I want to do with my life? Would I be happier out in the world, among many kinds of people, working and teaching?"

Teresa sat still, her head bowed and eyes closed.

"This is wonderfully done, my dear." Diana patted her arm. "I'm impressed."

"Will we have time to talk about this? Maybe it's too long?"

It was 10:45 A.M., and they were supposed to finish by 11:00. They rarely ended on time, and unless she had another appointment, Diana didn't care. She enjoyed working with her students; she would never push them out the door nor charge them for extra time.

She continued to read:

> "Finally, the day came, and the doctor told us that Mama could come home. I packed my things, said goodbye to my friends and teachers, and traveled by taxi to my mother's home, the home of my birth."

Teresa was at her side, seeing how much further Diana had to go.

"Yes, yes, it's almost the end," she told her.

Suddenly, the front door opened, and Mark came in, slamming the door behind him. The two women looked up.

Mark walked down the hall, not saying hello, or "sorry to interrupt," just staring at Diana. "I'm expecting a package from UPS. When it comes, call me." He turned around, ran up the stairs to his room, and quickly came back down. "You can phone me," he shouted, then left the house with another door slam.

"Rude son of a bitch!" As she said this, Diana reached for Teresa's arm. "You don't have to say that too often, in either language."

"Oh, Diana. That is not a nice young man."

She sighed, then continued reading.

> "My mother came home. A nurse came to help me during the days. At night, I slept near Mama's bed, waiting for her to move, to maybe need me. I never slept too well. I prayed for her to become better, but God had another plan.
>
> "In two weeks, while she was being washed by the nurse, Mama had another stroke. This time, she did not recover. She died that same day, right in our house, with the doctor and nurse by her side. I was very sad, but after all the waiting, I knew God had given me the answer. I would not go back to the convent; I was to do His work on the outside. I thanked Him then, and I thank Him to this day."

Diana put the essay aside. She felt chills, which was always her reaction when something she read especially touched her.

"Excellent. I'm so proud of you."

Teresa sighed. "I always wanted to write about this but never did. I'm happy you like it."

They went over the grammatical errors and discussed better word choices. Overall, it was probably the best writing Diana had seen from her.

The telephone rang—an unknown number.

"Pardon me," Diana said and took the call. "I do have a room listed for the fall, yes," she said, as Teresa watched." After a pause, she added, "No, I can't take cats. So sorry. Good luck finding a place."

She hung up. "That's the only call I've had today, except for the woman coming over later."

"You could rent many rooms, my lady," Teresa said. "Maybe I should move in here too? Have my teacher right in the same house? I could help with the cleaning, the cooking. . . ."

Diana laughed. "And keeping some of these other tenants under control; making the ones who don't behave follow the rules."

"Yes. Of course. I could do that."

"My dear, we will probably continue to get along and be good friends if you have your own space to live and work."

"*Si.* I mean, *yes.*" Teresa picked up the essay. "If I could speak to people like Emily the way I can write this, I would be much happier with myself." She frowned. "Or if Emily and other people were more like *you*, I would not be so afraid all the time."

"Do you have an extra copy, Teresa? I want to keep it in my files."

"Of course. Here it is. And I take your corrections. Thank you."

"Thank *you.* This is a gift." Diana held up the two pages. "When you get upset with yourself, why not remember when you were not afraid? Remember Open School this spring? Wasn't that a good experience?" She wanted to get in some conversation before they ended the class.

"I told you how scared I was before that time?" Teresa looked alarmed, as if Ms. Emily might be hiding somewhere, listening.

"And how did you handle your fear?" Diana sat back down at the table and gave Teresa her marked-up essay.

"I decided to be strong. I am the teacher, right?"

"Correct." Diana grinned. "You *are* the teacher."

"I was very prepared."

"You were very *well* prepared."

"Yes, I was very well prepared. When the parents began to come into my classroom, I welcomed them like they were my family."

Teresa stood up and pretended she was in the classroom, greeting the parents:

"How do you do, Mr. and Mrs. Abbott? Do you want to see what Melissa has been working on this term?"

Diana listened and watched as Teresa sat back down at the table and moved her papers around.

"Your daughter is doing wonderful work," I say to them . . . *said* to them. "Tell me, do you know Spanish?" She paused and then continued. "Please sit down right here, and we will have a brief lesson. That way, you will understand what Melissa is doing in this classroom."

Teresa clapped her hands. "They love it."

Diana held up her hand. "Past tense. That was last May. They *loved* it."

"I give . . . *gave* . . . all the parents a Spanish lesson. Not one of them know . . . *knew* . . . Spanish!"

Diana slapped the table. "By George, I think she's got it."

Teresa beamed. "They received so much information. And, later, they all shook my hand and told me I was a very good teacher." She sighed. "That was a big success, Open School Day."

"I love to hear that story," Diana said. "If only you could keep remembering how confident you felt on that special day."

"I was not confident. I was so frightened before they come . . . *came* . . . I thought I could not do it."

"But you *did* do it. And you'll do it again." Diana realized she was part teacher, part therapist for Teresa. She didn't have this same deep relationship with her other students.

You do what you have to do, she realized. If Teresa improved and got over her fear, that would be a real gift. Money aside, the feeling that she had helped was an extra reward for this kind of work.

"Now, for your writing assignment next week, I have another one-worder. Do you want one?"

Teresa's eyes widened. "It depends. What's the word?"

"Listening."

She nodded. "I get that. And should I listen to the convention? Make it political? Or to other news, from this country or others?"

Diana smiled. "That's up to you. "Listen to yourself and to things outside yourself. However, you interpret that. Maybe you can find some humor in what you write down."

"Unlike what I write today, yes?"

"What you wrote is so important to you. I know you can also write light or funny. Just go with what inspires you."

"Okay. I will do that."

Chapter Six

Frank's new 2008 Honda Accord sedan, silver blue and shiny, pulled into the driveway. He had bought it in July after his other Accord hit the 175,000-mile mark. "It's a good car for a journalist," he had told Diana. "I have to do a lot of driving."

What is he doing here?

"Excuse me," she said to Teresa as she walked down the hall to open the door.

"Surprise!" Frank grinned and gave her a quick kiss on the cheek.

"Yes, indeed. A surprise."

"I figured you might be done by now." He gestured toward the dining room as he handed her *The East Hampton Star*, just out today. "There's a review of that show last Saturday night; your volunteer night?"

Diana took the paper and nodded. She was a docent at Guild Hall, and the local papers always wrote reviews of the John Drew Theater events.

Wally was barking and jumping on him, his tail wagging. "Hi, big boy," he said to the dog.

"We're almost done." Diana led him inside. "Teresa, this is my good friend, Frank."

"How do you do."

Teresa nodded and took out her purse. She pressed a few bills into Diana's hands. "I will see you in two weeks, okay, darling? Next week is so busy, with the first week of school and with my sister here from Mexico."

Frank walked to the refrigerator and helped himself to a cold bottle of water.

"Where do you live in Mexico?"

"She lives in Guanajuato."

"And where is that exactly?"

Teresa hesitated. "North central part of the country."

"It's considered one of the most beautiful places in Mexico," Diana said.

"The home of San Miguel de Allende?" Frank asked.

"Yes. Such a lovely town, with historic, old buildings; the tourists love this."

"I'd like to visit," Frank said, "and maybe take your teacher here with me."

Diana and Teresa both smiled, and Teresa gathered her papers and prepared to leave. "I haven't seen my sister in two years."

"Write about that if you want." Diana stood up. "Or get her ideas on 'listening' and write something together. Make it fun. Does she speak English?"

She gestured. "*Un poquito.*"

She seemed to wait for disapproval, but Diana patted her shoulder. "Don't worry, be happy," she said.

Teresa extended her hand to Frank, "So nice to meet you."

"Likewise." He held onto her hand and gave a little bow.

Diana and Teresa hugged. "I call you." Teresa hurried out the door. "Maybe you come and meet my sister?"

"That would be delightful."

Frank sat down at the dining room table.

"Well, you're looking handsome this morning," Diana said. His white hair was newly trimmed, and his blue cotton shirt set off his summer tan.

"How nice. A compliment!"

She shrugged and busied herself with her papers. "Obama will be giving his acceptance speech later, as you know. I'm looking forward to watching that."

"Yeah, me too. And most of the country." He stood and walked around the room. "I went to the thrift shop," he said. "Got a couple of antique frames I can fix up. Couple of old tools, too."

"You and your thrift shops and yard sales. You could open your own store with all that stuff you have." Diana was amused as she put her books and papers on a pile to the side of the table. "Want some coffee or tea?"

"When is she coming?" Frank pointed to the ceiling. "Our Polish beauty."

"Noon. We have a while."

"I'll have tea, I guess."

While she was in the kitchen, Frank walked into the living room. "Why do you keep subscribing to *The New Yorker*? It takes forever for you to finish reading them." He picked up several issues that were on the coffee table.

"Why do you subscribe to *Sports Illustrated*?"

She brought his tea to the table, along with a fresh cup for herself, and then set out a bowl of diced watermelon and cantaloupe, along with two small serving bowls.

Frank chuckled. "Because of the Swimsuit Issue, why else?"

"So the point here is . . . what?"

He shrugged. "Just having a conversation."

Diana narrowed her eyes. "And criticizing me."

He laughed out loud. "Goddamn it, woman. We talk like I'm married to you. Do you realize that? This is the way an old married couple would talk."

So true, Diana thought. She glanced at the photo of Gary over the fireplace. He resembled a young Spencer Tracy from the early 1940s when Tracy acted with Katherine Hepburn in *Woman of the Year*.

Gary gave her the photo, taken by a photographer friend of theirs, for Valentine's Day, along with a vase of a dozen long-stemmed multi-colored roses.

Frank looked nothing like her late husband. What they had in common was that they were both decent, intelligent, loving men, men she could respect and trust.

"It's awfully crowded in the village right now," he told her. "A lot of folks will be getting parking tickets. The rent-a-cops are out there, doing their jobs. I tried to go into Waldbaum's to buy a few things, but I didn't bother. I'd have to park too far away or risk getting one of those tickets."

"The walking would be great exercise." Diane pushed the bowl of fruit toward him. "Have more. It's good for you."

He grinned. "Okay, Ma," and spooned some into his bowl.

"Good boy." She helped herself to the fruit, too.

"Hey," Frank said, picking up *Hamptons Magazine* from a nearby table. "Want to do this? Go to the Hampton Classic?"

"Talk about crowds, Frank—are you serious?"

"We park in the field in Bridgehampton, walk a distance to the seats—walking would be great exercise, Ma." He mimicked her. "Then we enjoy the show. See all the beautiful horses and their beautiful riders."

Diana laughed. "I haven't gone to the show in years. You're right. It could be fun."

"We'd see local celebrities. Christie Brinkley, maybe; Alec Baldwin? Jerry Seinfeld? Even Mayor Bloomberg. His daughter, Georgina, is always in the competitions. He shows up for her."

"I'd want to sit near them, Frank. Up in a VIP tent where I know there's shade and good food. We could talk about politics. The Mayor is an Independent, as you know. We'd talk about the Democratic Convention."

"So I should call Bloomberg and get us invited?"

She nodded. "Tell him you're a journalist, and you need to observe him close up."

Frank laughed. "Along with fifty other journalists, right?"

"And their assistants, including me." Diana grabbed her paper and pen. "And it would have to be this afternoon. I'm busy for the rest of the week."

He looked at his watch. "Too late to call the mayor. Or any of the other big shots. Damn!"

"Good idea, though," Diane told him.

Basia's yellow Beetle raced into the driveway, followed by a blue van. Her boyfriend, probably, helping her move.

Diana stiffened. "Party time," she said. "I'll bet you came here so you could ogle this pretty young thing."

They both watched as Basia and the van driver looked around, surveying the grounds in this neighborhood, before heading for the front door.

Frank sipped his tea and sighed. "Tenant number 752. Here we go again."

RULES FOR TENANTS:

No cooking, please, if I am teaching, or if I have guests.

Chapter Seven

Mark would be moving out in four days, on Labor Day. Last week he told her that he had found a room in Hampton Bays—the land of the drinking and hot babes.

"But you work not far from here, in East Hampton," Diana spoke as courteously as she could manage. "That's a lot of driving. A lot of traffic, too."

"They charge half of what you charge," he told her, not as courteously.

Half of the off-season rates? She wondered. *What did you get for $400 a month*? Maybe his new house was filled with drinkers, druggies, babes, and if he was lucky, a designated driver.

"That's nice," was all she said and didn't pursue a conversation. Why get annoyed again?

Diana studied Basia now, quite a hot-looking babe herself. She wished she had a camera as she watched Frank's eyes sparkle as he followed her new tenant move around.

"This is Steve." Basia pointed as her boyfriend followed her up the hall stairs. He was tall and thin, with dark brown hair, and wore metal-rimmed eyeglasses.

"Hello," Steve said, gasping under the weight of one of Basia's cardboard boxes. They made at least ten trips up and down.

Once, when the two were resting outside by their cars, Diana ran upstairs.

"Oh, my God!" She said it so loud that Frank climbed up after her.

"Everything okay up there?"

Then he saw it, too. "Holy shit."

Basia had moved so many boxes, large plastic containers, and clothing on hangers into the small room that there was barely any room for her to move around, no less, sleep there. There were piles of linens tossed on the bed—pillows, blankets, sheets, and towels.

And she had brought still more stuff upstairs and down to the basement, which Diana offered as extra storage space.

"Oh sure, I have plenty of room down there," she had said earlier.

She watched Frank's deadpan expression as she said it, after introductions had been made. He didn't offer to help them but did say, "Watch that you don't hurt yourselves."

"I am a masseuse," Basia told him. "I am strong." And as soon as her arms were clear of stuff, she handed him her business card: "Basia Godlewski, Massage Therapy. Call anytime."

Frank smiled and put the card in his shirt pocket. "Thank you. You never know when we might need your services, dear."

Was he trying to flatter the young woman, or was he flirting?

"That's so true," Diana said, holding her own card. "We'll have to keep these on our refrigerators."

Frank caught the sarcasm, but Basia was apparently unaware of the slight.

"I am very good at what I do," she said as she hauled yet another huge plastic box down to the basement. There was no more space upstairs, perhaps not even for Basia.

"We are almost done," she said to Diana. "Soon, I can relax."

"You sure have a lot of things." Diana pointed to all the cartons still in the hall.

"Oh, I have much more. I bring later."

Frank looked at Diana and grimaced. They walked out to the rear deck, where she slumped down into one of the cushioned yard chairs. Frank threw a ball into the yard for Wally, who charged right after it.

"Remember Veronica, that yoga teacher, a few summers ago?" she asked.

"The dame who gave you the money upfront, then canceled the check without telling you? Man, I think you wanted to kill that one."

Wally was back with the ball, so Frank tossed it off into the bushes.

Diana nodded, recalling how she hired a private detective to find out where Veronica had moved so she could serve her with a summons. She was determined to retrieve her money. Finally, she called, and they settled out of court, with Veronica paying for the detective and $1,200, or one month's rent.

"Bye-bye," Basia called to them. She waved the house key that Diana gave her earlier. "I see you later."

She backed quickly out of the driveway, narrowly missing the neighbor's van parked in the street.

"I should go home," Frank said. "I'm working on the book again."

"Your family history." She got up, deadheaded a few geraniums, and threw them in the trash can.

"Right."

"You've been working on that for a long time."

"I started it once I moved into the cottage, not long after Louise and I separated. Lots of research. Lots of interruptions."

Diana nodded. "I'd like to read part of the book."

"Sure." He paused. "That's the first time you ever asked to read it. Do you realize that?"

"Maybe I can be helpful, having been a librarian?"

"I'm sure you can."

Diana pointed to the upstairs windows. "I really do hope that Basia works out. She hasn't even spent a night here, and I find her exhausting."

"Remember two years ago, on Labor Day weekend?" Frank patted her hand. "Those two people who called you on a Saturday?"

"How can I forget? They were coming for two nights. And they gave me their credit card number. I figured Evelyn could run the card at her B&B. She referred them to me, after all, and said she wouldn't mind."

Wally raced to the fence, barking furiously at a squirrel in the yard, running to a tree.

"You get him, Wal." Frank clapped his hands. "I wonder what he'll do if he ever catches one of those critters."

"The couple never showed up." Diana had dialed the number in her caller ID, and there was no answer. No answering machine, either. "Damn!" She frowned. "It wasn't even a real number."

"Conniving bastards," Frank said, scowling. "Basia's got to be better than that."

"She's staying for more than a weekend," Diana reminded him. "And she hasn't paid me what she's supposed to."

Frank was petting Wally, back now from his near-encounter with the squirrel. "And you haven't forgotten the criminal lawyer who freaked you out a few years ago?"

"Boris. As in Karloff. It was for a whole week, July 4th through the following week. A defense attorney, he told me. So strange-looking, with those deep, dark eyes and pale skin. And quiet. He gave me the creeps."

"A man who appreciated great literature, right?"

"I couldn't believe it when I went up to give him fresh towels. Those titles! *Final Truth: The Autobiography of a Serial Killer; The Mormon Murder: A True Story of Greed, Forgery, Deceit, and Death; Son: A Psychopath and His Victims.*"

Frank laughed. "You called me in a panic." He raised his voice. "'Would you mind coming over and sleeping on the couch, Frank.' Such a scared little girl."

Diana hit him on the arm. "And you wouldn't come here."

"I thought about it," Frank said, "but I was on deadline, and a friend was coming to visit. I worried about you, though."

"That's comforting." Diana stood up and pointed to the gardens. "It's so beautiful out here, isn't it?"

"I know you love it."

"I do." She looked at the clock. "Are you staying for lunch?"

He got up from the chair. "No, but thank you. I've got chores to do before I go home to write. How about a movie tonight? We could get a burger or something and catch a film while the Polish princess is settling in."

"Oh no, this is the big night in Denver. I want to hear Obama speak."

"True. Me, too. I could come over here."

"Let me think about it."

He walked inside the house before walking to the front door. Wally followed him, his tail wagging. "Later, fella."

Next, he was in the Honda and out the driveway. Diana could hear the car radio, tuned to the convention update probably. The news guy was listening to the news reports.

Chapter Eight

Diana made herself lunch. Thin slices of ham on toasted whole wheat with lettuce and tomato. Some honey mustard and mayo. The tomatoes were excellent this year, and the fruits and vegetables came from local farms—another blessing of living on the East End. She should make a list.

When they first moved out from Queens, neither Gary nor she knew if they would like living in the Hamptons full-time. How could they know? Until then, it had been weekends and summers for her, with Gary staying in Queens during the week because of his job. It couldn't be the same as full-time.

While she ate, Diana read through *The East Hampton Star*. Besides the Hampton Classic all week, there were gallery openings, concerts, plays, readings; so much going on for the holiday weekend, the last hurrah before summer rentals ended and families returned to the city with their kids.

Tam, her Vietnamese ESL student, called earlier. Her husband had met her in her country while on business, married her, and brought her to the U.S. She couldn't keep their appointment tomorrow. Her husband and she had unexpected guests who would stay for the weekend.

"That's fine, Tam," Diana told her. "Have a great weekend. Enjoy yourself."

She remembered the first summers after they moved to East Hampton and before they took in summer tenants. There were calls from relatives and friends who wanted to spend time visiting them in the Hamptons. They would come, stay overnight, on the sofa, doubled up in one of the kids' rooms, or on the air mattress in the basement, and go to the beach all day.

Gary and she would remain at the house, cooking and cleaning up after them. In some cases, they would lend them a car. Usually, no one offered to pay for the food and drink.

"Good thing we're rich," Gary joked. And they'd think of places they might travel to on future weekends, figuring they'd save money by not staying home and entertaining all the summer guests.

If he could see her now, the landlady she had become, what would he think? Would he be like Frank and tell her to move on, to move out?

Brett called from his office to ask if Basia had arrived. "She sure has," Diana said. "I wonder what you'll think of her."

"I'm leaving in a couple of weeks," he told Diana. "It's more important what *you* think of her."

"I didn't get the best first impression, to be honest. She's tough; could be a con artist."

"You'll find out soon enough."

"I'm probably just nervous. Too many awful tenants this year. . . ."

"I beg your pardon?"

"Oh, stop. You're perfect," Diana said. "You and your tiny dog, Buster."

"You bet your boots we are. Want to take a walk downtown tonight?"

"Frank may come over to watch the Democratic convention. This is the last night."

"Isn't Monday your weekly date night with him?"

"Yes, we had dinner then."

"Well, if your boyfriend, Frank, doesn't show up, and you don't want to watch all those speeches, let's go out walking, okay?

"My other boyfriend."

"Correct. And we can take the dogs and have a nice conversation. Maybe stop at Babette's for a snack."

"I'll call you later."

"Okay. And cheer up, landlady."
"Right."

Diana was going to turn on the stereo, but, no, she wanted some quiet time to sort out her feelings. As she cleaned up the kitchen—her dishes and cups and those of Teresa and Frank—she thought of calling her daughter or son to say hello. But no, it was Thursday; they were probably at their jobs. She didn't want to make a call, only to hear, "Can't talk now, Mom. Sorry."

Later, she would call, or the kids would check in over the weekend.

Jennifer lived in Portland, Maine and Dennis lived in Seattle. It made for pleasant traveling, going from one coast to the other during the year. And, usually, both kids came to East Hampton during the Christmas holidays. Diana hoped that they would give her grandchildren as her friends' children did. But then she'd be sorry they lived so far away.

Jennifer almost had a baby but lost it two months into the pregnancy. A year later, when she was 28, she and her husband broke up. No re-marriage; no more children. Not yet, anyway. She had a good job, working in management for L. L. Bean.

Diana smiled as she looked down at her light green T-shirt. From the store, of course. One of many L. L. Bean gifts from Jennifer.

Dennis dated and even got engaged once, but his girlfriend wanted to wait. She wasn't sure marriage would be right for her. Maybe he, too, would surprise her in time, with a wife and kids; even step-grandchildren or adopted would add to her life and, hopefully, to his. He had a new girlfriend now, another "techie" he met at his job at Amazon.

Both kids were still young enough to bide their time and make good choices about whom they married. *And I'm still young enough to be a good grandma,* Diana thought.

She walked over to the sofa, grabbed the yellow and red throw, and lay down on the plush red pillow.

"I'm so tired," she said to Wally, who followed her. "I need to rest. Too much excitement." They could go for a nice walk at the beach later when it cooled down outside.

Diana patted his head. The dog sniffed close to her face once she was lying down and quickly dropped to the floor beside her.

"That's right." Diana sighed. "You take a nap, too. Good boy."

It was cool and quiet; no tenants or students. No Frank, no anyone. "Thank God," she mumbled and gave in to the overwhelming feeling of exhaustion. *No talking. No thinking.* She quickly drifted off to sleep.

RULES FOR TENANTS:

No noise late at night (music, TV, talking) Preferably not after 11 p.m.

Chapter Nine

A half hour became two hours. The front door banging shut woke her. Diana was in such a deep, peaceful sleep that it made her jump. Basia?

It was Mark.

Wally did not make any sounds when Mark came into the house; he merely wagged his tail. He liked Mark and followed him into the kitchen, where Mark noisily pulled a Corona from the refrigerator, took a bag of chips from the closet, and ripped it open. He did a loud clearing of his throat as he noticed Diana on the sofa; he was on his way to the hall and the stairs.

"I'm gonna pack up some of my stuff," he said, not looking directly at her. "I'm leaving a couple of days earlier. Anybody using the washing machine?"

"It's all yours." Diana got up from the sofa and tried not to scowl at him. It was almost five o'clock. "I'd appreciate it if you'd dust and vacuum before you leave, Mark. That's what everyone does."

His room was a mess of sweaty clothes, empty beer bottles, and overflowing trash cans; she dreaded having to go in there and clean up after him.

He frowned. "That's the landlady's job, not mine." He walked into the hall and stomped up the stairs.

"Idiot," Diana muttered. Wally came to her side. "We should get out of here for a while. The idiot will be up and down the stairs the next few hours."

She washed, got dressed, and led the dog out to the car. It was cooler outside now, maybe 70 degrees, not humid, and she packed two bottles of cold water, one for each of them. His dish was in the car. It would be pleasant down at Maidstone Park. It was too early to go to the ocean beaches. No dogs were allowed until after 6:30 P.M. She often drove down to Main Beach out of season and lined up with the other cars to watch the sunsets. Wally could run in the sand then and into the ocean waves.

Diana drove north on Three Mile Harbor Road, down into Springs, and turned left on Flaggy Hole Road. There was a deli on one corner, the beach sign on the other. Then she drove down to the park.

Wally paced the back seat of the car, whining.

"You know where we're going, don't you, baby?" Diana turned to face him.

He sniffed through the rear window that she left halfway open.

She drove past Michael's Restaurant, where Gary and she used to meet friends for dinner. It had a simple menu; seafood and meats and delicious desserts. They had a good time on those nights out, as a couple, or with others joining them.

She drove down and around the beach area and parked the car near the jetty. This led to the wide, northern stretch that flowed, eventually, into Gardiner's Bay. Cars filled the parking lot. Summer was ending; the tourists and the locals all wanted to be at the beach.

Diana loved to walk with Wally on the hilly, paved road that circled the beach. It ran through a long wooded preserve, past acres of beach grass near the shore. There was a ball field too, and picnic areas. A dog park had opened off Three Mile Harbor, on the non-beach side, where many people liked to walk. She went there a few times, but it was just acres of shrubs and tall grass, with about a half-mile-long lap circling throughout the park. No hills or water views, no sandy beach or seagulls.

Fishing boats, sailboats, and yachts came in and out of the harbor. Fishermen were down on the beach, and picnickers were spread out on blankets and chairs at the beachfront. Young guys in pickup trucks were hanging out in the parking area, smoking and talking. One of the trucks had a "For Sale" sign in the window.

Whenever she saw a large red pickup like this one, Diana remembered that Gary had been dead less than a week when she decided to sell his truck. The monthly payments were high. She didn't need a truck. As Gary's caretaker, she hadn't been able to work for months. The hospice aides came every day, but she had to be with him day and night. She *wanted* to be with him. After taping a "For Sale" sign in the truck window, she parked it near the street and sold it the same day.

The water was calm; the sky blue with a few white, puffy clouds. Diana got out of the car and breathed in the fresh, salty air. Bayberry, beach plum, dune grass, goldenrod, and heather surrounded her. Beyond the shrubbery was the sandy beach. The scene was a living postcard. She had been coming down to this beach for all the years she lived in East Hampton. There were weekend visits, with Jennifer and Dennis, when they were growing up, and with Gary, even after the kids went off to college. Right now, being here felt like a precious gift.

Thank you, God, she thought. *Thank you for reminding me how extraordinary this place is.*

Wally jumped down from his seat and followed her along the paved road. Suddenly, he leaped into the brush, like a deer, and disappeared, only to come out about 100 yards ahead of her, waiting for her to catch up. "I'm coming," Diana called out, laughing. "You're too fast for me!"

Some dogs played near the water, and Wally took off through the seagrass and sand to get acquainted. One of the dogs, a golden retriever sitting next to a fisherman, was covered with sand and soaking wet. After jumping up and down together, Wally and the retriever raced into the water.

"Watch my lines!" the fisherman yelled.

Diana ran toward the water. "Move!" She shouted and waved her arms.

"Thanks," the fisherman said. "Don't know that they'll pay any attention."

He wore waders and a cap that had West Lake Marina stitched on it.

"You fish in Montauk, too?"

"Oh, sure." He smiled. "Anywhere they're runnin'."

Gary used to take the kids out to Montauk, to the main dock on West Lake Drive, to teach them how to fish. They were eight and ten years old. When they brought home the afternoon's catch, they were so proud. Diana cleaned the fish and breaded them, sautéing them in butter, serving them with mashed potatoes, local corn on the cob, and maybe homemade coleslaw.

Wally raced out of the water, shook himself all over Diana, and ran back in. "Yikes!" She started laughing. "What did you do that for you . . . you *dog*!"

She tossed her sandals in the sand, rolled up her pants, and waded into the cool water. Maidstone was not a sandy-bottomed beach; pebbles and rocks and shells had to be contended with, mostly round and firm to her feet, and she always picked some to take home.

For the moment, Diana felt blissfully removed from the house and tenants. She didn't care about her feet.

> "I must go down to the seas again, for the call of the running
> Tide is a wild call and a clear call that may not be denied . . ."

Ah, John Masefield's "Sea Fever," one of her favorite poems.

If only I could hold onto this moment and call upon it when I get frazzled at home, she thought.

Diana sat down near the water's edge, on a large piece of cardboard she found in the road, and surveyed the beach dogs at play. Wally walked along the wet sandy shore with his new friend, sniffing at seaweed and clam shells and other delights. Another dog joined in, and soon there was a fourth. These two, a cocker spaniel and a border collie, had run down from the paved road to play while their owners looked on. Diana waved to the people; she recognized them from previous walks. They waved back.

Some of the picnickers also seemed familiar. *I probably could walk up to them, introduce myself, and join their parties,* Diana thought.

"How's life?" she could ask. "Have you had a good summer?" Or, "Are you staying here through the fall?"

Many people who lived out here had two homes. In an ideal universe, maybe that's what she would be doing herself: vacating the house for part of the year and living elsewhere. It wasn't the first time she had contemplated this as a way out of the world of tenants, but she had never tried to make it happen. *Still a possibility*, she thought.

Wally ran up to her, sandy, wet, and panting, and plopped down next to her, his legs crossing over hers, and put his big soft head in her lap.

"Tired puppy," Diana said, stroking his head. "And we haven't even had our walk yet."

"Between the dance exercises and walking the dog, you should be good for another 25 or 30 more healthy years," Frank told her early in the summer. There was admiration in his voice.

Frank. She reached for the cell phone in her shirt pocket and dialed his number.

"Hi, it's me."

"Well, dear lady, did you have a nice afternoon?"

"I did. I am. I'm down at the beach, and it's gorgeous."

"You should have called me earlier," Frank said. "I would have joined you."

"Sorry, I didn't think of it." That would have spoiled her calm mood, Diana knew. Frank would have talked about practical matters: her past and present, her future—the whole landlady business again.

"What about tonight? Want me to come over and watch the convention?"

"Frank, I'm very tired. I'd rather wait and get together after the weekend. Is that okay with you?"

"Sure enough. I'll watch Obama, like everybody else. Democrats, anyway. Let's get together Monday night, even though that's Labor Day. Call me if you need any help with *Miz* Basia, okay?"

"I'll do that. Bye." She stood up, brushed herself off, and checked her watch. Six-thirty. "Okay, Wally, it's time for our walk."

Some people were packing up their picnic gear, while others seemed so content there on the sand that they might well stay until after dark. The parade of boats entering the harbor, on their way to the docks south of here—Harbor Marina, Shagwong, and Halsey's, among other marinas—continued. Sailboats, their masts lowered, sports fishing boats, large and small, and yachts were lovely to watch as they drifted by, some people waving their hands from the boats and the shore.

Because of the holiday weekend, many of the boat owners had come out earlier. Since the weather forecast was excellent, they would have several good days on the water. Gary and she had talked about buying a boat. But it was never the right time to buy, or it wasn't the right boat. They had plenty of opportunities to go sailing and fishing with neighbors and friends, so it wasn't something they missed.

As they started up the southern side of the road, Wally stayed close by her side. "Are you too tired now to run through the woods?"

He usually took off through the brush and brambles, unleashed and adventurous, enjoying his private paradise.

To her right, through a clearing in the nature preserve, she saw the osprey nest atop a tall pole on the other side of the inlet. She looked closer, wishing she had her binoculars. Were the birds still in the nest? Or did they finish their job of hatching the chicks and teaching them to fly before taking off? The osprey couple usually arrived in mid-March and left for South America in early September. This pair of large hawks, with their dark brown-and-white wings, had been coming here for many years.

Gary used to walk this road with her. Diana remembered how he pointed out Mama Hawk, the larger bird, atop the nest, and Papa Hawk, dive-bombing into the water and coming up each time with a fish.

Sometimes they would take the ferry over to Shelter Island, where there was a row of nests near Ram Island. They could even hear the baby hawks' little peeps. Afterward, they would have lunch or dinner at the Ram's Head Inn. The dining area and terrace stretched out across the lawn down to Coecles Harbor, and guests would be sitting in white Adirondack chairs on the sloping lawn.

"We should celebrate our anniversary over there," Gary said once. It was in mid-September, and they would stay at the Inn. Spend the weekend, hike once through the Mashomack Preserve, and be pampered with great meals and good wines at the Inn.

"It wasn't meant to be," she muttered. Wally looked up. "I'm not talking to you, sweetie." Diana looked down at him. "I don't see our big birdies. Or their babies. They may have all flown away."

She stepped back onto the road. "Let's keep walking."

Her cell phone rang, and Diana knew who it was.

"I don't know if I want to go to the village tonight, Brett. I'm walking now. I may be all walked out."

"I have to work a while longer," he said. "You don't have to tell me now."

She continued the familiar route up the road leading out from Maidstone Park before crossing over to the left, then onto the wide grassy field that led to another picnic area. This one was in the woods east of the beach. A group of soccer players, Latinos from the community, were running through the ball field in the distance, tossing the ball, shouting in Spanish, with a group of onlookers laughing and cheering.

Diana put Wally's leash back on. They kept walking until they came to the road near the picnickers that led back to the beach and, after a long stretch, to where Diana had parked the car.

"Time to go home, my boy," she told him. He jumped up on the car seat, panting, and quickly sprawled out to rest.

They drove back to the house. She fed Wally and the cats and made a tuna fish salad sandwich on whole wheat bread, with lettuce and tomato. Out on the deck, she sat, sipping at her glass of cream soda. Heaven. The sounds of traffic drifted across the farm field, and she listened as more tourists drove into East Hampton for the holiday weekend.

How wonderful to be right here, Diana thought, spreading her arms wide. *Brett will have to walk without me.*

She turned on the TV eventually and watched the convention. It was being held tonight at Invesco Field, and the news would report, on Friday, that there were more than 84,000 people in attendance. Before Obama, the numerous speakers had included former Vice President Al Gore and the governors of Virginia and New Mexico. It wasn't until 9 P.M. that Obama took the stage. Music played in the background as the cameras circled the standing audience, hands waving and applauding, voices shouting as Obama tried speaking above the din:

"Thank you . . . thank you so much . . . thank you, everybody . . . thank you . . ."

On and on, he went, smiling, glowing, for close to three minutes, as his admirers kept on clapping and whistling. Diana timed it, her face flushed from smiling. She now wished that Frank or Brett, *someone,* was here, sharing this with her.

Coincidentally, it was the 45th anniversary of the Rev. Dr. Martin Luther King's "I Have a Dream" address on the mall at the Lincoln Memorial in Washington, which Obama referred to near the end of his long speech. He said it was that American spirit and promise that continued to push us forward and bind us, even through uncertainty.

He spoke of immigration and early pioneers in the country, "that American promise" that helped workers stand up for their rights and for women to "reach for the ballot," and said that would lead us into the future.

Earlier in the evening, before Obama's speech, Rep. Luiz Butierrez of Illinois spoke, asking his friends in the Latino community, in the immigrant community, to please join him in voting. Barack Obama was the change we needed, he told the audience, and would always stand up for justice for all Americans.

When she first decided to tutor foreigners in English, after leaving the library, Diana had placed a small ad in *The East Hampton Star*. She posted fliers at the local business service, in the bookstore, the library, and in several delis. The reaction was immediate.

"I like to learn English. You teach me how?"

"My brother and me, we need to know English. When we can see you?"

Many people, mostly Latinos, contacted her. But Diana stuck to her rule to only work with foreigners who had graduated from high school, and preferably from college, in their countries of origin. She wanted to discuss literature, politics, art, ideas with her students so that she could listen and learn from the experience, too. During her library years, she had interacted with so many foreigners and enjoyed it.

"You should be a teacher," her co-workers told her more than once. She was singled out as the staff interpreter, though she didn't know any foreign language too well.

Just *un poco* Spanish, *un peu* French, *ein bisschen* German.

"To be a teacher in the right sense is to be a learner."

This quote, by Kierkegaard, hung over her desk.

Another, by Einstein, was in the kitchen:

> "It is the supreme art of the teacher to awaken joy in creative expression and knowledge."

In June, Diana was asked to tutor a French woman staying with her sister for part of the season. The sister's home was a huge mansion on the ocean in Sagaponack. Diana tutored her in the playroom, a room larger than her own entire first floor. She would drive down to the ocean three mornings each week, wedge her car between those of the beachgoers trying to find a parking space at Sagg Main Beach, and park in a shaded area on the estate.

They became friends, Dominique and Diana, and she had an invitation to visit her new student in the French Alps. Gary and she had traveled years ago to the Swiss and German Alps, but not to the French region. She would plan a trip for the winter perhaps, or next spring. Maybe she'd even take a French conversation course during the fall.

She let Wally out one more time, then settled down with him and the cats, ate a small slice of pound cake with fresh strawberries and cream, and her nightly cup of tea. After tidying up the kitchen, she went into the bedroom, a book in hand, and settled into bed.

"C'mon, guys, you can join me," she said, as all three pets climbed up to join her. As on most other nights, she would read until she fell asleep.

Chapter Ten

Jennifer called on Friday morning. "Did you watch the convention, Mom?"

"Oh, sure. Not all of it. It was on every day, all day."

Her daughter laughed. "Yeah, I know. I watched what I could whenever I had time."

"The Republicans start their convention on Monday. Right on Labor Day."

"Yes. So how are you, Mom? Are you all set for the big weekend?"

"I suppose. It's only Friday. You know what it's like out here in summer, especially before and during the holiday weekends. I'd like to hide out in the house, but I do have a couple of places to go on my list."

"I hear you." Jennifer sighed. "We've got lots of tourists here, too. Maybe growing up there prepared me for living in Maine?"

"Could be. I enjoy it better when I visit you in the fall. It's so peaceful."

Diana had slept well. Watching the convention held her interest, and later, there were no noises from upstairs, no nightly visits by tenants to the kitchen that she could hear. Airplanes started flying over the house early in the morning, and helicopters headed to and from the East Hampton Airport. For this last big summer weekend, any way tourists and second-home owners could get here—by car or bus, train or plane, motorcycle or boat, maybe even by walking or hitchhiking—they were on their way.

"I may be in Manhattan around September 15," Jennifer said. "A few of my college friends are meeting up. If I can't come out east, maybe you could meet me in the city for lunch or dinner."

"I'd like that. Take the Hampton Jitney, catch up with you." It was either drive into the city and find somewhere to park, like a garage, take the train, then cabs, or ride in on the Jitney, the high-end bus that took people from the end of the North and South Forks of Long Island to and from New York City each day.

"You could stay here if you want. I'll have my own room at the hotel. Extra bed."

"A pajama party?"

"Yeah, right."

"Well, let me know. And enjoy yourself this weekend. You have plans?"

"We're invited to a party in Kennebunkport." With her boyfriend of the last six months, Diana knew. "It's on a huge sailboat. Should be fun."

"Have a good time, honey," she said, and after hanging up, she watered the few indoor plants—the two orchids, her large peace lily, and the aloe, plus the African violets Dennis sent for her birthday. Outside, she did some more watering. The pink roses along the side fence were still blooming, and Diana trimmed off a few to take inside.

During the night and morning, she dreamed of—what else?—tenants: the good, the bad, and the ugly.

> "There are two kinds of people in this world, my
> friend. Those with loaded guns and those who dig.
> You dig."

Diana remembered this dialogue from her librarian days, researching the Sergio Leone film from the 1960s that starred Clint Eastwood and Eli Wallach. She wasn't a fan of spaghetti westerns, but it was fun to learn about them and share the information. So many of those old reference questions and answers just stayed in her head.

One of her really "good" tenants, Roseanne, a graphic artist from New York City, went to the movies with her when she lived here. The Sag Harbor Cinema showed a lot of foreign films that appealed to both of them. Their evenings usually included dinner out in Sag Harbor, at Conca D'oro, The Corner Bar, or maybe the Dockside. If it was a clear night, they'd walk through the village after the movie, looking in the shop windows, and head down to Long Wharf. In the warmer months, enormous yachts were docked there, on both sides of the wharf, the wealthy owners sitting on the decks, their servants moving back and forth with cocktails and hors d'oeuvres.

"Ah, the good life," Roseanne said more than once, waving to the deckhands.

Sometimes they waved back, or bowed, which made us laugh.

They had many pleasant and intelligent conversations during her stay. *Where was she now?* Diana made a note to call Roseanne. *Maybe we can get together sometime in September.*

She set the sprinkler in the middle of the yard and turned the faucet on at the side of the house. The grass, moss, and garden areas would get a good soaking before the day heated up.

"Oh, you love that, don't you?" Wally ran in and out of the sprinkler, and it reminded her of the kids, when they were young, on hot summer days. "Silly dog! I'll have to dry you off before you go inside."

Other good tenants were Simon and Patrick, who came after Roseanne and lived upstairs at the same time. Simon was from London and was an art historian. Patrick was a carpenter and worked for a local building contractor.

"Can I help you fix that, Diana?"

"How about if I build you a fence around those garbage cans?"

Patrick was always offering to do work around the house, not expecting payment. For the few large jobs he did, such as building that fence and fixing a leak in the shed roof, she insisted on paying him. "Oh, you don't have to. Honestly, it's okay."

But he'd take the money with a shy grin.

Simon was an urbane, blond, handsome guy in his late twenties, educated at Cambridge, with a charming British accent. He was quiet when he was at home, spending minimal time in the kitchen, as did Patrick, with pastimes that included running, biking, and reading in his off-time when he wasn't working at the Parrish Art Museum.

Eventually, Simon moved into the city to work at another museum, and Patrick found love; he got married and moved out. Patrick stayed in touch for a few years, as did Simon, but both young men eventually disappeared from her life. Diana felt fortunate to have met them and to have had them in her house.

For brunch, she prepared an omelet, breakfast sausages, and toast. After feeding Juan, Cassie, and Wally, she sat at the inside table near the window, propped up *Dan's Paper*, a thick, Labor Day weekend edition, and started to read.

"Behave, guys," she said, but they were busy eating and didn't pay any attention.

The humorous but phony "Police Blotter" *Dan's Paper* published each week reminded Diana of still another tenant, Gerard, a "bad" one, who arrived one January day, addicted to painkillers, which she, of course, knew nothing about. Gerard, she would find out, added vodka to the daily mix. He was a short, plain-looking fellow in his mid-forties, out of work on disability, he told her, but "I plan to be back in that job, or another one, before too long."

They went to dinner one night, to Sam's in the village, for pizza, and Diana noticed a small flask that he took from his pocket when heading for the men's room. She didn't comment on it or ask, "What's in the bottle, Gerard?" She was his landlady, not a detective, although, in retrospect, she wished she had been.

"I have a Master's in Civil Engineering," he told her during dinner. "I want to take it easy for a while, give my health a break.

That's why I decided to leave the city and spend some time out here in the Hamptons."

He had a spinal injury that he eased with oxycodone, although Diana didn't learn what medication he was taking until it was almost too late. In the large bedroom, Gerard had set up bookcases he brought from the city, filled the shelves with all kinds of reading—scientific to business to travel to mystery novels—nothing too literary. He positioned the TV near the end of the queen-sized bed in the room; that way, he could rest all he wanted and needed without moving around too much. Diana had a bed tray table, similar to that in a hospital and gave it to him.

"Gerard? Are you in there?" Sometimes, when she heard no noise at all coming from his room for a whole day and night, she would knock on his door.

He was sleeping, or he was reading. He always kept the door unlocked, but she didn't want to open it, to march in and check on him.

"I'm fine, Diana," he said once, with a big smile, when they were face to face. "Just resting up, like the doctors told me to do. Soon I'll be up and around and ready to dance."

He did a quick hip hop, blew her a kiss, and shut the door again. "Good night."

"He makes me uneasy," she told Frank during their Monday night dinner date. Gerard had been living in the house for less than two weeks. "I don't want to be his caretaker, but that could happen."

Frank thought the new tenant was nice enough, educated, well-mannered, plus he certainly seemed able to pay the rent. "He's lucky that you look out for him," Frank said. "He seems to be one of the better ones that landed on your doorstep."

"I'm not so sure."

Gerard was her only tenant at that time, and he rarely used the kitchen. There was a toaster oven in his room and a small refrigerator that he stocked with soda, juice, water, whatever he needed. He also had a shelf with grocery items, plus a table and chair.

Three weeks into his stay, things turned "ugly." After another silent day and night, with no footsteps overhead, no TV noise, no sign of activity whatsoever, Diana climbed the stairs one afternoon and knocked on his door.

"Hello?" she called. "Are you all right?"

Silence. No reply. She knocked again. "It's me, Gerard. Is everything okay?"

Diana felt tense but did some slow breathing and tried to remain calm. She would have to do what she had resisted so far: barge in and make sure he was conscious. *Alive.*

"Come in." The words were faint and hoarse. There was no other noise, or she surely would not have noticed how he spoke.

"Are you okay, Gerard?"

She opened the door, forced a grin, and walked to the end of the bed, where he was sitting up against pillows, his head slightly bent, with half-opened eyes, barely moving.

"Oh, I'm hanging in there," he said, an expression he used quite often.

"I was getting concerned. You've been unusually quiet up here."

"Just relaxing."

Diana looked around for signs of pills, needles, whatever he might be using. "Do you need anything?"

"No. No, I'll be okay. It takes time. . . ."

The words came out slowly, in almost a whisper.

"Gerard, I forgot to ask you for an emergency number. I ask that of all my tenants. A relative or employer, in case I ever have to contact someone."

He nodded slightly. "Yeah, sure. I can't get up right now. My brothers live out of state, as I told you."

"Is there anyone else?" Diana could feel her stomach churning; something was terribly wrong here.

"I have a cousin," he mumbled. "He lives in Southampton."

"Could I have his name?"

"Tommy. Tommy Brewster."

"Brewster. Okay. Is he in the phone book?"

"I think so."

"Well, that's good. I'll make a note of it."

Gerard nodded, smiling slightly. Then he closed his eyes. "Got to sleep."

Diana turned to leave. "If you don't mind, I'll want to check on you again."

He didn't answer. He was out.

Downstairs, she dialed Information, and, sure enough, Thomas Brewster of Southampton was listed. Diana wrote down the number.

The phone rang, and it was her friend, Evelyn. Her bed and breakfast in town was quiet this winter, with few guests. "How are you doing, Diana?

"I'm so glad you called." She tried to relax, but her breath was labored. "Could you come over here? I mean, right now?"

"What's up?"

"My new tenant. He's sick, unconscious almost. It might be drugs."

"I'll be right there."

Evelyn hung up and came within ten minutes. Ten minutes in which Diana walked up and down the stairs several times, listening at Gerard's door but not opening it, dialing Tommy Brewster's phone number but hanging up before anyone answered.

"Tell me what you think," Diana said, leading Evelyn, a dark-haired, petite woman wrapped in a warm, blue quilted coat, up the stairs. "Should I call 911?"

She opened the door, and Gerard was in the same still position, asleep—or was it not just *sleep*?

"Call," Evelyn looked frightened. "This guy is out of it, I'm sure. Let the medics take care of him."

"Thank you, my friend." Diana hugged her. "I would have called for help, but you've made me extra sure I'm doing the right thing."

The police and ambulance came quickly. Gerard was barely responsive. "Good thing you called us," one of the EMTs said.

The crew worked on resuscitating him before moving him onto a gurney, bundling him up, and taking him to Southampton Hospital. Evelyn left, and Diana called the cousin. He wasn't there, so she left a message.

By the next day, she would find out, as would the cousin and the rest of Gerard's family, that he almost died. The combination of alcohol and drugs in his system was so high that "it's a miracle he pulled through," as Tommy Brewster told her when they spoke on the phone.

She put *Dan's Paper* aside and cleaned up the table and kitchen and, smiling, watched her dog and cats stretched out on the pet cushions on the floor. "What a life you guys have!" She listened to Wally snore as he rolled over.

Gerard stayed at the house for several months after being released from the hospital. She tried not to mother him or be his nurse, but Diana was relieved when he told her he was moving to Minneapolis to live near his brother.

"I still dream about him," she told Evelyn long after he was gone. "I hope he's okay."

RULES FOR TENANTS

Please be considerate of others.
Clean sink, mirror, toilet,
and tub regularly.

Chapter Eleven

She looked through the mail; the bills could wait until after the weekend. There were discount cards from Macy's and from the car dealership, plus notices from the New York Public Library and the World Wildlife Fund that her yearly memberships were up for renewal. A Horticultural Alliance meeting would be held in mid-September.

In her bedroom/office, Diana filed the mail in her "Pending" manila folder in the file cabinet. She took a thick one out marked "Photos." Recent pictures of Jennifer and Dennis, last year's Christmas family photos, plus pets, garden, beach, friends, travels; it was time to sort through these and maybe put them into albums. There were already a dozen of these on the bookshelves.

"I'm tired of creating more and more albums," she told the kids last December when they visited. "They sit there on the shelves, and what for?"

"So you can look at them if you decide to write about us," Dennis said, joking.

"Or do a documentary," Jennifer laughed. "Maybe Frank can help you with that."

"So that should be my new year's project?" Diana asked.

Soon everything would be digitalized, they assured her. All photographs would be on the computer.

The computer . . . she turned it on and checked for emails. More news about Obama's nomination, of course, with news of the upcoming Republican convention.

Her friend, Shona: "See you soon, dearest. Meet you at the Reservation entrance." Her reminder of their date at the Shinnecock Pow Wow tomorrow.

Dennis: "Hi, Mom. Sorry I missed you. I'll give you a call on Saturday or Sunday. Have a great weekend."

A few announcements and invitations for events coming up in September in the city and on the East End,

"Yes, I'll see you at the gate," she replied to Shona. "How could I forget?"

"Okay, Dennis," she wrote next. "Call when you can. XXX"

Wally walked up to the desk, tail wagging, and Diana patted him. "C'mon, let's take a walk, okay?" She put on sandals, took the dog leash from the hall table, and led him out the front door. "I can use the exercise, too," she said, heading down the path toward the street. There were no sidewalks here, only a stretch of town-mown grass on either side of the road, next to the canopy of tall trees in this heavily wooded area of town.

They walked past a neighbor's house, set back from the road like her own, that Diana knew had been rented for July, and to another tenant, for August through mid-September. Frank had told her they made "big bucks" doing so. Of course, he suggested that she do the same: rent out for the season, go away "somewhere nice" then come back; she'd have the whole house to herself during the next eight or nine months.

"Plenty of people do that out here," he told her, as if she wasn't already aware of this.

Diana knew lots of stories about renting whole houses. Seasonal tenants who were responsible and took care of homes as if they owned them. And others who rented, calling the owners if the slightest thing seemed amiss. But there were different stories: overcrowding, loud parties, damages inside and outside the house.

One friend, who moved away a few years ago, had a "perfect" rental family one summer who rented their house again the following year. This time, the tenants decided to turn off the dehumidifier in the basement, only God knew why, causing incredible damage from mold.

Diana sighed. "We're in our house, Wal, and we'll probably *stay* in our house."

Cars passed as they walked, but very few compared to those on Montauk Highway, two miles away. Traffic could be heard in the distance, a remote version of the Long Island Expressway, as she sometimes thought of the highway when the cars and trucks were non-stop on this busiest of summer weekends.

The Long Island Railroad was across the fields, and that, too, sent sounds across the farm fields as trains arrived and departed. The whistles blowing in the night were sounds that brought her back to the years she had grown up and lived in Queens.

Wally led her onward for about half a mile, but eventually, she turned him around to go back to the house.

"So what do you think?" Diana looked at Brett, who had finally met Basia in the upstairs hall this Friday evening before the young woman took off in her car.

Brett looked handsome in his yellow shirt and tan slacks. "Aside from the fact that after we said hello to each other, she said, '*Vood* you mind keeping the toilet seat down in the *batroom*?'"

Diana chuckled. "Good for Basia. You're spoiled; three guys living upstairs all summer."

"I guess she's attractive, in that blowsy, Eastern European way."

"You're an authority on such things?" She laughed.

"I have a keen sense of beauty. I know it when I see it."

"Of course you do! And where are you off to tonight, oh wise one?"

"I've got a date. Will you keep an ear out for Buster? He's tired out, but he might miss me."

"You mean you're going on a date with someone other than me?"

Brett smiled. "You had your chance, woman. I asked if you wanted to go for a walk, didn't I? You blew it."

Diana laughed. "Go. I'll take care of Buster."

Frank called while she was polishing her nails, preparing for the pow wow tomorrow. Later, she would shower and wash her hair.

"So now we have a woman running for Vice-President. What do you think of that?"

"I don't know much about Sarah Palin, Frank, except that she's a Republican and the governor of Alaska. I figured you could tell me."

"Well, it's a surprise to most people. Obviously, it's an attempt to get the women voters."

She laughed. "And it might. Look at all the people who'll be afraid to vote for an African American."

"It should be an interesting fall, with all the political news."

"Right. The Repubs and Dems trashing each other."

"Let's hope it's not too sleazy."

"Agreed. Talk to you over the weekend."

"Okay. Have a good night."

"You too, my lady."

Chapter Twelve

"Here is the rent money," Basia said on Saturday morning.

Diane held up the slim envelope. "Is this for the whole two months?"

"No. It is for September only." She shrugged. "It is best I can do."

"I must insist on having two months' rent. First and last, as I told you several times."

Basia looked at her watch. "I have appointments in Sag Harbor, my private clients. We can talk about this later?"

"You will have to borrow the money if you don't have it. Maybe you can put it on your credit card."

"I don't have credit card," Basia replied.

"You *must* pay me this week." Diana tried not to raise her voice.

"Okay, okay," Basia opened the front door to leave. "I go to rob a bank. Maybe my boyfriend will help me." She reached over to kiss Diana's cheek. "You're a very nice woman. Don't worry."

Off she went. *Don't worry. Be happy.* Diana fell back into the sofa. "Help me, God," she said to the ceiling. "Should I throw her out now or wait until later?"

Mark had left Friday evening, grumpily accepting the check Diana gave him for his security deposit when he moved in. He didn't say good-bye and, sure enough, left it to her to clean up. She started by bringing down the small trash pails and linens and spraying the room—bed, drawers, closet, and rug—with disinfectant.

"I'll have the room nice and clean for you by tomorrow morning," Diana told Basia, who had been up and down between her bedroom and the laundry in the basement. Since she arrived on

Thursday, Basia must have done six loads of wash. At least she got her to stop using "Bounce" in the dryer. Basia put aside her usual brand and bought a fragrance-free type of detergent. Well, almost fragrance-free. Diana decided not to carp about it.

"You don't have to clean." Basia brought her own bucket, mop, paper towels, and Swiffer duster into Mark's room. "I used to be cleaning woman, you know. I don't mind doing work in here. I work fast." Basia accepted Diana's cleansers, her Comet and Windex and Pledge, with a big smile. "I do this later when I'm home from my job."

She didn't mind if Basia wanted to help clean the room. It was probably her way of justifying not paying the two months' rent upfront.

It was a cloudy day, around 70 degrees but humid. Diana, dressed in a white skirt and sandals, and a V-neck bright blue cotton top, drove to Southampton to meet with Shona and two of her friends. Every Labor Day weekend, a small group of women met up at the annual pow wow on the Shinnecock Indian Reservation. This pow wow was one of the largest Native American gatherings on the East Coast. A three-day event, it hosted over 100 Native American arts, crafts, and food vendors from all over the Americas.

Shona, tall, dark-skinned, and buxom, was a librarian, and Diana and she used to work together. She was part Shinnecock and part African-American and had grown up on the reservation.

"I'm so glad to see you," she told Diana.

Diana hugged her.

Shona's friends, also from the area but not from the tribe, shook her hand and exchanged hugs. Then the four of them ate a lunch of corn chowder, made by the Shinnecocks, and shared a plate of their fried crab cakes and clam cakes.

"Oh, I missed this," Shona said. "A whole year since we've eaten such food. Super delicious."

"Yes!" Diana and the other women nodded happily.

Afterward, they walked over to watch the tribal musicians and dancers on the enormous stage erected in the middle of the grounds. This year, among the foreigners, there was a family—a mother, daughter, and son—who had traveled from Australia.

"They're performing some of the aboriginal Dreamtime dances," Shona said.

Huge crowds of people swayed in time to the beat; the entertainment was virtually non-stop. Most of the music included drumming and, no matter where they walked, drums were beating in the background.

The singing was mostly chanting, in various Native American languages, and there was a high-pitched screech that accompanied the voices. It was so much like what Diana saw in the cowboy and Indian movies when she was growing up.

The Lakota Sioux had a stand where they sold buffalo burgers and lemonade.

"Shall we?"

All four of them ordered lemonade; they were too full for the burgers. They also had to pass up the wonderful fry bread with various fillings.

"Let's take some of that home later," Shona said, and they all nodded.

It was a hot day, and Native Americans crowded the grounds, many in their tribal costumes, and tourists surrounded the stage and roamed the grounds.

Shona's brother and cousin were performing in both a drumming group and a singing group. Diana and the others stood close to the stage to watch them. They had seen the groups last year and were happy to see them again. "Talented family you have," Diana said, or shouted, as Shona clapped and waved her arms.

To the far rear side of the stage, she noticed a group of four men playing drums and dancing in small, slow steps. One of the men kept looking over at her. Like the others, he was dark-skinned and had jet-black, straight hair. He was naked from the waist up, wore a silver chain and a turquoise and silver medallion on his hairless chest, and had streaks of red paint running down his face. Unlike the others, who seemed very serious about their dancing, he was smiling. Actually, he was smiling at her, and she found herself smiling back.

"Where are they from?" Diana asked Shona.

"I think they're Sioux," Shona replied, "from out west."

When the Sioux finished dancing behind the stage, the smiling one took two bottles of cold water from a table and walked toward Diana. The dancing on stage had ended for the moment, and Shona and her friends headed toward the vendor tents. They wanted to see the Indian jewelry and handicrafts, such as blankets, beadwork, small drums and wall hangings made from animal hides, and the native art.

Diana paused. "I'll be along shortly," she called after them.

Shona winked at her. "See you later, pretty lady."

"I enjoyed watching your performance," Diana said, shaking the tall guy's extended hand. She didn't know what to say exactly. This was her first real Indian, other than Shona and the other Shinnecocks, many of whom were mixed races. She'd met Native Americans during her travels, of course, in upstate New York, Arizona, California. She couldn't recall a single one-on-one extended conversation, however.

"I'm glad you enjoyed it." The Indian handed her a bottle of water. "That was just a rehearsal. We'll be up on the stage soon."

"I'm Diana," she told him, accepting the cold drink. "Thanks."

"Tom," he said, taking in the whole scene. "This is a great turnout. These pow wows are so much fun; I get to so few of them, unfortunately."

"Tom?" Diana grinned. "As in tom tom?" She pointed to the drum at his waist.

He laughed. "Tom Eliot. But my Indian name is 'Spirit of Great Owl.'"

"Where are you from, Spirit?" Diana asked, following him to a bench at the side of one of the dance circles.

He laughed again. "I knew you had a sense of humor. Something about your facial expressions while you were watching us and the other dancers."

"Is that a compliment?"

"Absolutely. Where are you from?"

"No, I asked first."

"South Dakota. Rapid City. I'm a lawyer there."

"You don't live on a reservation?" Diana noticed his bright dark brown eyes and nicely curved eyebrows.

Tom smiled. "Half the Sioux, if not more, don't live on reservations. There are natives all around the country, too, full breeds and mixed, who don't live on reservations. We've been assimilated into the mainstream of society, or so we're told."

He gulped at his bottle of water, and Diana noticed his prominent Adam's apple. He was slim and wiry and *looked* Indian. *Of course,* she thought. *That's what he is.*

"You live out here, Diana?"

"Yes. In East Hampton. I was born and raised in Queens, however. One of the boroughs of New York City?"

"Yeah, I know. I make business trips to New York. I land at JFK or La Guardia. You ever been to South Dakota?"

"No, I haven't."

"You would love it. People come from all over so they can camp in the Black Hills or in Badlands National Park. I'm from the Oglala Sioux tribe. Our Pine Ridge Reservation covers some 3,400 square miles, and I live about 100 miles from the center. Beautiful country."

"I guess I'll have to put that on my to-see list," Diana said. "You know, *1,000 Places to See Before You Die*?"

"Yeah. This place was on *my* list. I've never been to the Hamptons before."

She glanced around. "This reservation is not typical of the Hamptons. You'll have to explore more of Southampton and farther east."

Sitting there and talking with Tom, Spirit of Great Owl, it occurred to her that this could solve her problem with the tenants: she could move to South Dakota and pitch a tent or a teepee. It would have to be large enough for her and Wally and the cats, of course. And it would have to be heated. If it got unbearably cold in the winters, she could travel farther south or pitch a tent or teepee somewhere in Southern Indian Territory.

"Come out to visit, and I'll show you around," Tom said. "Our annual Black Hills Pow Wow is held in mid-October, right there in Rapid City.

"I just may do that." He was flirting, Diana knew, and she was flirting, too. "Do you live in a house out there, Tom?"

"Ah!" He nudged her arm, his bare, dark skin touching hers. The scene was getting downright erotic. "You have a picture of me living on the rez, don't you? In a tent!"

Looking down, she replied, "Yes, I guess I do. The way you're dressed and all. It's hard to imagine you probably don't walk around dressed like this all the time."

He sighed. "I left the reservation as a child; got a good education. There's a great deal of poverty among the tribes, unfortunately. But I had a different kind of life. I live in a real house, all mine. I'm single for many years now, went through a divorce. Two grown kids. One grandson. The house is paid for, cared for, and waiting for me to come home."

Diana nodded. "We have similar situations, two kids, a single house owner. A widow. Only I don't have to travel so far to get back home."

"Why don't you give me your email address?" Tom's group was back, and it was time to perform.

"Yes, okay. I've got to meet my friends over there"—she pointed—"and maybe buy myself a nice turquoise ring before I leave this afternoon."

As soon as she said this, he removed a turquoise ring from his pinkie finger and placed it on the ring finger of her left hand.

Diana looked down, her eyes wide, then stared at him. "Does this mean we're engaged, Tom?"

He laughed. "Well, you have to promise to watch us dance. And you have to learn about Native Americans and the Sioux culture. You seem like an educated woman."

"I was a librarian; I teach English to foreigners."

"Should be a breeze for you!"

"I'll wait for your email." Diana stood up. "It's been a real pleasure meeting you and becoming engaged to you, Tom."

"Likewise." He leaned over and kissed her on the cheek. "Maybe next time we meet, it will be in Rapid City."

"Yes, or at another pow wow."

Diana smiled as he walked away. You leave the house, she thought, and you never know who you'll meet. So many times, men stopped to chat when she was walking with Wally. Nice fellows, all ages. But she wasn't open to flirting; maybe she wasn't ready for a new relationship, or maybe she needed someone like Tom, Spirit of Great Owl, who was direct and came on strong. Too bad he lived so far away.

I will not let this be a problem, Diana told herself. *I did that once before, and it hurt. It took a long while to get over Kenneth.*

With her friends, she watched Tom's group perform on the big stage. The dance and music riveted her, but, of course, she focused mainly on Tom, on her new "fiancé" who danced and drummed and sang, or chanted, right near her several times. She danced along with the crowd, swinging and swaying with the beat, and her friends joined in, moved by her enthusiasm and obvious joy. When the performance was over, just before his group left the stage, she gave Tom a big wave. He threw her a kiss.

"You've got a hot new man there, girlfriend," Shona said, smiling, as she led Diane and the others away from the stage.

"Do you believe this?" Diana raised her head, did a silent "whoop," and clapped her hands. "He's so nice. My first Native American."

"You might have to write about this for 'Modern Love'."

Diana nodded. "Or if I get rejected, I'll try *American Indian Magazine*. You know, from the Smithsonian?"

Shona laughed. "Only a librarian, other than well-educated Native Americans, would know about that one."

They followed their friends to one more stand, the Cherokees, where they ordered small containers of bread pudding, served warm and coated with maple syrup.

"Amazing," Diana said. "I'd love to have this recipe."

"Want to ask?" Shona said. "Maybe they'd give it to you.

So she did, and the woman at the stand graciously told her how to make the pudding. She would cook it at home and think of Tom.

They left the pow wow shortly afterward.

"Keep me posted about you know who," Shona said in the parking lot, gesturing toward the stage area.

"Of course." Diana smiled and hummed Indian chants, or what she believed they sounded like, all the way home.

RULES FOR TENANTS:

Keep dirty laundry in your room.
Clean dryer filter after every use.

Chapter Thirteen

When she walked into the house, Diana could tell that Basia had been extremely busy during the afternoon. More cartons and large, black plastic bags were stacked in the hallway. Out in the yard, Basia had strung a new clothesline between two trees, over which a white quilt and two sets of pink bras and panties fluttered in the light summer breeze.

"She has no class whatsoever," Diana grumbled as she patted Wally's head.

Down in the basement, another surprise was waiting. Basia had done more laundry, emptying Diana's damp load from the dryer and throwing it into a basket.

"Is this insane, or what?" She spoke to the dog, who had followed her down the stairs. "I'm calling that bitch right now."

But she didn't do it. It would be dark soon. She wouldn't have to look at the clothesline. If she did, she probably would run outside and cut it down. Leave the quilt, bras, and panties on the mossy lawn and let Wally and the cats roll around on them.

It had been a long, hot day. The talking and laughing and dancing had worn her out. A loud day, too, with the incessant drumming and chanting filling her ears.

All that plus meeting Tom and then driving home through traffic. Tourists had taken over this last summer weekend. The roads, of course, but the shops, the restaurants, the sidewalks, even the back roads. Home, at last, Diana wanted to enjoy the peace and quiet. Basia and her boldness could wait. Tomorrow she would talk to her.

She ran the dishwasher, then caught up on the daily news on the television. She wondered what Obama was doing now that the convention was over, where hurricane Gustav was down in the Gulf of Mexico, and what the Republicans were preparing in Minnesota.

After the news, she read some of her book, *The Year of Magical Thinking*, the memoir by Joan Didion. She had hesitated to read this about Didion's life before and after her husband died, thinking it might depress her. As the reviews said, it was an amazing work of literature: journalistic, precise, clear language, just like all of Didion's previous non-fiction.

Diana couldn't identify with the author's story, although it made her feel very sad for Didion. Her husband, the writer John Gregory Dunne, had sat down with her to have dinner, suffered a massive coronary, and died. Didion wrote:

> "I only remember looking up. His left hand was raised and he was slumped motionless. At first I thought he was making a failed joke, an attempt to make the difficulty of the day seem manageable."

Gary had rarely been sick during all the years of their marriage. Suddenly, he had pains in his upper abdomen and a burning feeling in his stomach that wouldn't go away. He made an appointment to see the doctor. It took four months for him to die, a quick, painful deterioration typical of Stage IV pancreatic cancer. His doctors prescribed anti-anxiety medications, antidepressants, and pills to help him sleep.

Didion's husband died instantly.

> "You sit down to dinner and life as you know it ends."

That was how she opened her first chapter.

For months after Gary died, Diana experienced that feeling. She would sit down to eat, or shop for groceries, or walk into the downstairs sickroom to check on Gary and life as she had known it was over.

Her husband wasn't there, and she used to tell Frank and her children, "*I'm* really not here sometimes. I don't know where I am."

They had rented one room out each summer, Jennifer's former bedroom. It was Gary's idea. The first time it was to a guy he knew, an accountant from his years as a CPA. It worked out well, so they decided to keep renting; the extra income paid for some expenses around the house and toward vacations. They took winter trips: a road trip down the east coast to Florida, a ski trip to Vermont. And in the fall and spring, road trips to upstate New York and to the Berkshires.

By April, when it seemed near the end for Gary, she had asked their latest tenant to leave. He was a nice man, a physical therapist from the city, who was renting the smallest of the three bedrooms year-round. He was only there on weekends so he could see clients. But Jennifer and Dennis would be coming again to see their father. Other family members, too: his sister and brother, a cousin.

Diana needed the extra space. She also felt she couldn't deal with a stranger living in the house. It was too personal, this tragedy; she needed to feel in control. A hospice nurse, an aide, and a social worker were at the house almost every day. When it grew dark, and she was alone with Gary, she was frightened. He moaned with pain and cried out in his sleep.

She shopped for groceries, walked the dog in the village, took the household trash to the dump, filled the car up with gas, and had it serviced—all chores they used to share. Now, these became Diana's responsibilities. She resented it at times. It was selfish on her part, no doubt. She had to keep saying to herself: *He's dying; you get to live. Stop with the self-pity!*

Their marriage was mostly a good one. They were supportive of each other, she felt, as far as their jobs and interests were concerned. Diana flirted with him less as the years passed, which he chided her about, but sometimes sex was spontaneous. They'd cuddle in bed, and both of them would approach lovemaking in a relaxed, gentle manner. The sex was good, she felt, as good as it would get.

They had arguments, periods of not speaking to each other, like all other couples. But they came together and made up and didn't let the arguments take over their lives.

Reading Didion's book brought back all these memories. Fortunately, Gary died while both children were at his side. The wake and funeral followed, with relatives and friends attending; so many tears and so much sorrow. Besides the eulogy that Frank gave, some six or more others stood to say kind words, including one of Gary's landscape clients, who was going to plant a tree in his honor. The children spoke, as did Diana's in-laws; all heartfelt and sweet comments and memories.

Then it was over. After the burial, which was at a local cemetery they had agreed upon, the children returned to their lives in Washington and Maine. Everyone else said their goodbyes and were gone. There was no more Gary to worry about and take care of, and no more tenants.

> "Life changes in the instant."

Another of Didion's opening lines.

He died in early June. Before they left, Jennifer and Dennis insisted on paying for a service to clean the entire house thoroughly, top to bottom.

"Rent the rooms for the summer, Mom," they told her. "It will keep your mind occupied, and you'll also make some money."

Didion had quoted from an article on "happiness":

> "It takes the average widow many years after her spouse's death to regain her former level of life satisfaction."

Like Didion, Diana couldn't decide if she was an "average" widow. And what, exactly, was her former level of life satisfaction?

She signed up with the Chamber of Commerce as a bed and breakfast soon after Gary died. There were paying visitors all that summer, pleasant people who mostly came only for weekends. It turned out, as her children had hoped, to be an extremely good distraction.

She logged onto her computer before going to bed. There was a message from Frank:

"Hope you had a great time at the pow wow. Call me tomorrow."

And, surprise, an email from Tom:

"I think you're right. I have to travel farther east of the Shinnecock rez, so I can experience this beautiful area you call home. Could I meet with you on Monday, late afternoon, after we're finished here?" He signed it, "Tom 'Spirit' Eliot."

Diana quickly replied:

"Hi, Tom. I'm imagining you sitting with your laptop in a teepee at the reservation, in your dancing outfit. How did Native American tribes ever manage before the invention of the computer? How did any of us?

"I'd be delighted to see you Monday. Call me before you drive out." She typed in her home phone number. "Here's my address. I can give you directions later.

"All my best, Diana 'Student of Sioux' Watson."

She whooped and hollered and did a little dance around the desk, glad that Basia and Brett were not home.

"Damn," she said aloud. She should have bought one of those Pocahontas-type cowhide dresses she saw at the pow wow. On Monday, she would wrap a band around her hair and stick a feather in it. She had one in the house.

"It means good luck," Brett had told her when he gave it to her last month. "It's from an owl."

An owl! She had forgotten that detail. She quickly Googled for "feathers as good luck" and found out that "Owls are thought to be messengers from the gods."

She sang as she shut down the computer:

> "I'm an Indian too
> a Sioux
> a Sioux . . ."

Diana took the Annie Oakley CD from its case, plugged it into the player, and listened as Ethel Merman sang the whole song from *Annie Get Your Gun.*

She danced around the bedroom, humming and smiling.

Funny lyrics! Indian names like Rising Moon, Falling Pants, Running Nose. Spirit of Great Owl was a much more dignified moniker.

Messenger from the gods. Was Tom really? And what was the message?

Wally and the cats were curled up on the bed, having watched her the past hour.

"Waiting for me, guys?" She joined them, claiming her side of the bed.

She was asleep before Basia and Brett returned home. When each of them came in, she woke up but went right back to sleep without any trouble.

The two cats remained curled up near her on the bed, and Wally stretched out on the bedroom rug.

Chapter Fourteen

Sunday morning, before Diana was even out of bed, Basia was up in the large bedroom, probably cleaning windows and dusting the furniture. The smell of cleansers was strong, and she could hear the vacuum. Brett had left to go to his office, taking Buster with him, as usual. The clothesline needed to be discussed, and the washing machine and dryer, but Diana felt relaxed and not in a combative mood. She dozed back to sleep.

The house was quiet when she woke again, so she got dressed and walked into the hall. She could hear Basia upstairs, talking on the telephone. Wally followed her into the kitchen, where she put the kettle on for tea. She fed Juan and Cassie and settled herself in the dining room to have a quiet breakfast.

She had just stirred sugar and milk into her tea when Basia descended the hall stairs, with loud and pronounced footfalls.

"Hi," she muttered, not looking at Diana. She walked quickly toward the kitchen, opened the refrigerator, grabbed her container of orange juice, and took a paper cup from the counter.

"Basia," Diana said, "we have to talk about that clothesline you installed in the yard. You put that up without asking me if it was okay."

"I had big fight with my boyfriend." Basia gulped down the juice. She wore a blue and white gym suit, white-heeled sandals, and her blonde hair was piled high on her head. Going to the spa, obviously. "He is son of a bitch, and I'll never speak to him again."

Diana sighed. "I'm sorry for your problem, Basia, but did you hear me?"

"Clothesline is not so important. I'll move it to another place."

"No," Diana said, "You'll *re*move it. *Today*. I don't want a clothesline as part of my view in the backyard. Also, would you please leave my clothes in the dryer? You took them out when they weren't dry."

"I am so sad." Basia stared now at Diana, teary-eyed. "My heart is broken, and you—you worry about a clothesline? You talk about laundry? Were you ever in love?" She pressed her hand to her chest. "Don't you remember what it's like? A broken heart?" She started to cry.

Diana got up from the chair. "Oh Basia, of course, I know how that feels. You poor dear." She sighed as she handed her a tissue.

Basia walked down the hall toward the door, the tissue at her eyes. "I have clients to see. I don't know how I will do my work."

Diana followed her, tsk-tsking, wondering if she would have to go outside and cut down the goddamned clothesline herself. Where had Gary kept the machete? He was always out in the woods behind the yard, chopping his way through the thick brush, making plans for still another garden that he hoped to plant one day.

Basia pointed up the stairs. "I clean so beautifully up there. You will please take a look?"

Diana nodded. "Of course, I will. Thank you so much."

Wiping away her tears, Basia said, "I have more things to put in your basement. Will that be okay?"

Suddenly, she was six years old, asking if she could bring over her toys.

"I guess so." Diana wondered, though, what "things" were coming next, and if the basement, which was the full length and width of the house, was large enough. "Sure."

"Thank you so much." Basia hugged Diana and kissed her on the cheek. "You are very good woman."

After she left, Frank called. "I was waiting to hear from you. Did you have a good time yesterday?"

"A great time. It was nice seeing the girls, and you know I like all the ceremonies and dancing."

"Big crowd again?"

"Thousands of people, it seemed."

"I've never gone, as you know. I'm surprised *Newsday* or *The Times* hasn't asked me to cover it or even to do a profile on someone from the tribe."

"It's worth seeing at least once."

"Yeah. Maybe I'll tag along with you next year," Frank said.

Fat chance, Diana thought. She'd be living in her teepee in South Dakota by then, studying to be a Sioux. She might even be married to one.

"I'm going to interview a guy who's visiting from North Carolina," Frank told Diana. "He's part of the Ross clan. I met him at the Long Island Scottish Festival in Old Westbury Gardens last year."

Frank had told her all about that annual summer event and even invited her to join him. It sounded like fun—the Scots and non-Scots, bagpipes, caber tossing, and highland dancing—all entertainment to promote Scottish history and culture.

"That should be an interesting interview. More information for your family history and the book."

"Yeah. We Rosses are everywhere. I'm getting to know them all. What about you? Have plans?"

"Teresa invited me to meet her sister." She looked at her watch. "That's at three o'clock."

"You should enjoy that."

"I will," Diana said. "They want to serve me Mexican desserts out on Teresa's patio."

"Nice. What about tomorrow night. Are we on?"

"I don't think so, Frank. Can we make it Tuesday or Wednesday? A friend at the pow wow has to leave the area on Tuesday. I'll be going out for dinner."

"Sure. No problem. It's your turn to pick the restaurant. Where do you want to go?"

"Let me think about it." If she didn't run off with Tom, she'd give it her attention. Right now, she wasn't the least bit interested in Tuesday or Wednesday.

RULES FOR TENANTS:

Chapter Fifteen

"The A/C is on, guys. You should be nice and comfortable."

Diana turned the television on at low volume for Wally and the cats before leaving. On her way to Teresa's apartment in Bridgehampton, she bought the Sunday *New York Times*, then stopped at the library to pick up the film, *North by Northwest*. Tonight, she would curl up with Cary Grant and Eva Marie Saint as they climbed Mount Rushmore.

"I'm so happy you came," Teresa said, squeezing her hand. "This is my sister, Cecilia."

"Pleased to meet you." Diana smiled and shook her hand. "There's a strong resemblance between the two of you."

Teresa translated this for her sister. "Resemblance is not an easy word," she told Diana.

"*Si*," Diana said. "*Hay semejanza.*"

"You're speaking Spanish!" Teresa hugged her. "I don't believe this!"

"*Ella habla espanol!*" she looked at her sister.

Diana laughed. "*Solo se un poco.*"

"*Si.*" Teresa turned to her sister again. "*Ella solo sabe un poco.*"

"Ladies," Diana said, "can we somehow just speak in English?"

"Of course. Cecilia actually knows some English. She will listen to us." She gestured to the patio behind the kitchen, where a round picnic table was set with a gaily-colored Mexican tablecloth. "Sit, please, with us. Cecilia has been preparing desserts all morning."

The air in the house was hot and filled with heavenly baking aromas. Diana was touched. They wanted to please her and to entertain her.

"We've been to Montauk to see the lighthouse," Teresa said. "I stopped at Ditch Plains, and they were surfing. So many people!"

"Oh sure," Diana said, "Summertime in the Hamptons. Of course, the surfers are out there a good part of the year."

"*Si.* Yes. I tell Cecilia about the Montauk Monster. You remember we spoke about this weeks ago?"

Diana nodded. "I showed you the photo that was in the paper. A young woman and her friends found the creature right there at Ditch. It might have been a raccoon carcass or a Pit Bull, but it was so composed that it's still a mystery." She paused. Teresa would have to translate all this for her sister. "What it was and now, *where* it is—someone took it away—will keep being a news story."

Teresa nodded. "We visited the dock there and bought fresh fish right from one of the boats."

Cecilia was smiling as she walked back and forth from the kitchen, bringing trays of still-warm pastries and cookies to the table. She set down a tall pitcher of iced tea.

"You like?" she asked shyly.

"This is perfect," Diana said, looking at the food and the setting. "It reminds me of a Mexican hacienda."

"It is, dear teacher," Teresa held her hand. "You are here! This is my hacienda, and finally, I get you to visit me."

"I also drove Cecilia through East Hampton," Teresa continued, "to see all the big mansions on Lily Pond Lane and those other beautiful roads. I showed her where Bon Jovi lives, and then we saw that house, Grey Gardens."

Diana nodded. She had shown Teresa those estates when they went down to the beach one afternoon. Cecilia now served them a variety of pastries and poured tall glasses of iced tea.

"We walked together on Main Beach," Teresa said. "I parked down near St. Luke's church in the village. I showed her Home Sweet Home, that very old house."

Cecilia smiled and nodded.

"We passed the swans and ducks in the Town Pond." She clasped her hands over her chest. "It was so beautiful. At the beach, we watched the people sitting on the sand and coming in and out of the water. A gentleman took our picture when I asked him."

"This is heavenly." Diana took a bite of a peach and cream-filled light pastry. "You are a wonderful baker."

Cecilia looked pleased, perhaps understanding.

"In Mexico, my sister bakes for her family and even for large parties. I have never learned to cook or bake as well as she does." Teresa sighed. "We have two different kinds of lives."

"I'm so lucky to be sitting here with the two of you," Diana said. "This is a charming patio and yard. You must enjoy it."

"I sit here sometimes at the table and write my assignments." She showed Diana her language books, which were on a nearby table.

After she ate two pastries, Cecilia was trying to give her still another. "No, no, I'll burst. Let me digest these first!"

"Diana *ha tenido suficiente.*" Teresa gestured for her sister to sit down and relax for a while.

"So tell me, dear teacher, what have *you* been doing this weekend?"

"Well, like most other people, I watched some of the Democratic convention."

"Oh yes, we too," Teresa said. "I like him. I like Mr. Obama. He should make a fine president for this country."

Diana looked up and nodded. "You and I met on Thursday." She sipped at her tea. "I've been busy ever since. One tenant left; another came in."

Teresa nodded. "Ah, yes. You were waiting for someone on Thursday to arrive."

"And you know I had trouble with Mark, the young man upstairs who was leaving."

"Yes. He made you so angry."

"Well, he finally left, and now I have a young Polish woman who moved in." Diana frowned. "She's already causing me problems. I don't know how it will work, having her living in the house. I have a feeling this may not last too long. She could drive me berserk."

Teresa grasped Diana's hand. "It's your house. If she makes trouble, you must say '*Vamonos.*'" Cecilia perked up at the word.

"Or you tell her, 'Hit the road, Jack.'" Teresa waved her finger. "You have trouble with her, you call me. I'll help you."

"You're a good friend." Diane held back a tear.

Teresa reached over to hug her. "Did you go to the Indian show?"

"The pow wow. Yes, I did. Yesterday. It was a wonderful afternoon." She looked at the sisters. "I met a nice man there, an Indian."

"Oh, teacher! You mean 'Native American,' not 'Indian.'"

"Okay. Okay, you can correct me. This is your house, after all." They laughed and held up their glasses in a toast.

"So tell me about this man. Isn't Frank your boyfriend? Won't he be jealous?"

"He's my friend, a very good friend, but not my boyfriend," Diana said. Cecilia was busy clearing the table of plates and napkins and the trays of pastries.

"In our family heritage, there are Indians. Chichimeca. It's in the history books."

"This man is a Sioux, and he's from South Dakota."

"That's so far away, isn't it?"

"I know," Diana said, looking at her watch and gesturing that she would have to leave. "Maybe nothing will happen, but it was nice to meet him and talk with him."

"Good. So you had a nice day yesterday, too. Tonight, Cecilia and I will see a movie in Sag Harbor. It's in Spanish, with English subtitles. Later we will go for ice cream down at Long Wharf. Tomorrow . . . I'm not sure yet about tomorrow."

Diana looked at the two women. "Tom—that's the Indian, I mean Native American, guy—is coming to visit me tomorrow afternoon."

"Aha! *El amor esta en el aire.*" Teresa and her sister beamed. "It's like a film, but this one is in English, no?"

"Yes. I mean, I guess so." Diana held her breath. "I've got to go home now. I enjoyed meeting you, Cecilia. And thank you for this." She held up the small white bag that held several more pastries.

There were hugs all around, with Teresa promising to call as soon as Cecilia left for home, so Diana and she could plan their next tutoring session.

It was about five o'clock and quiet in the house when Diana arrived home; Brett and Basia were out. The dog and cats welcomed her as she sat down in the cool, silent living room for a few minutes, petting them and assuring Wally she would walk him. She thought about dusting and cleaning the living room so it would look extra nice when Tom arrived. But, no, she would wait until tomorrow.

The bags and boxes were gone from the hall, and, curious, she climbed the stairs to see how Basia had settled in. Basia's door was closed, but the door to the small guest room was wide open.

"Whatever you don't want, put in the smaller room," Diana had told Basia, and her new tenant certainly took her up on it. The room was filled with all of the larger room's lamps, two tables, one chest of drawers, the television set, and all of the prints and paintings that had hung on the walls. Besides boxes and bags of Basia's belongings, two throw rugs were strewn across the white rocking chair Diana kept in there. On the twin bed, she could just about see her own folded linens: queen-sized spread and pillows; even the curtains, the white, lacy curtains. Didn't Basia want curtains in her room?

The door to the small room was open, Diana quickly realized, because it was blocked with "stuff" and couldn't be closed.

She opened the door to Basia's larger room and gasped. It was transformed. The down quilt that had hung previously on the clothesline was plumped up now on the queen-sized bed, which had been moved across the room and backed up against two windows. Throw pillows—gold, white, and tan-colored—were scattered on the bed. "Old master" paintings and faux golden sconces hung on the walls. A white "fur" rug covered one part of the floor; an oriental rug covered another. Swags of bronze-colored, shimmering satin fabric that hung down to the floor and were held open with elaborate gold metal clasps replaced Diana's white curtains. Behind the bed, a metal chain of wide, amber-colored candle holders was draped above the curtained windows.

On a black wrought iron table, opposite the bed, stood a larger television set, flanked by "antique" vases and bowls. The two double-wide closets were packed from top to bottom with Basia's clothing, shoes, bags, and cartons.

How had she managed to do all this in a few short hours? The woman was an Amazon! Did she own all this stuff before today, or did she go out and buy it? Everything in the room seemed like merchandise she regularly saw at T.J. Maxx. The place resembled a glittery, faux high-end home furnishings store. Maybe Basia couldn't pay all the rent because she went on a shopping spree?

"We're home!" Brett and Buster were downstairs at the front door. "Where are you, landlady?"

"Up here," she called.

"Checking on my room, are you? I promise to vacuum. I know there are dog hairs. I know." Brett and the dog ran up the stairs; He was about to kiss Diana but noticed Basia's makeover. "Holy shit! It looks like a bordello."

"A T.J. Maxx bordello." Diana sighed.

"The woman doesn't have very good taste, does she?" He examined Basia's artwork on the walls. "We could sell all of this stuff for about twenty dollars total. That is . . . unless we decided to take it to the dump."

Diana gestured for him to come back into the hall. "It's not right for us to be in her room, whether or not we think she has good taste."

"Maybe she's a prostitute?" Brett said. "Have you ever had one of those as a tenant?"

Diana laughed. "Not that I know about. Not one that worked from home, at least."

"Keep an eye on her. See if she wears revealing lingerie during the daytime, and watch out for any johns that may appear in the middle of the night."

"I'll do that." Diana pretended to be serious. "I'll call in the vice squad, if necessary. Does East Hampton have a vice squad? I don't even know."

"This is the Hamptons. It's a resort community. The tourists are supposed to have fun. Vice is probably fine with the cops."

"Okay, okay." Diana chuckled. "I'll let you know if we get raided."

"Buster!" Brett ordered the dog from Basia's room and into their own. "All we need is for him to pee on that white rug."

He looked into the small guestroom. "Hope you're not expecting last-minute guests."

Diana grimaced. "They'd have to sleep on the couch or on the living room floor." She started to go down the stairs. "I've seen more than enough. I think I'll hide in my room and say a few prayers."

"When you're done, want to go for a walk in the village with us?" Brett asked. "Maybe in an hour or so? Around 7:00? We could stop and have dinner. My treat."

"Well, that's quite an offer."

"My boss is giving me a recommendation for grad school." He clapped his hands. "A good one."

"Great work, my friend," Diana kissed his cheek. "Yes. I think we should go and celebrate that. You, me, and the dogs."

"It's a date." Brett gave her the high sign and retreated to his room.

In the kitchen, Diana made herself tea and toast. When she opened the refrigerator to take out the strawberry preserves, she was overcome with the powerful, gaseous odor of Polish sausages: kielbasa. There had to be at least three pounds of sausages and smoked ham on one shelf, wrapped in paper. Basia must have brought them from her previous house.

On Wednesday, when she first moved in, Basia had loaded the refrigerator with food; Diana noticed now that none of it was touched. Salad greens, slices of roast beef, a tomato, peppers, restaurant leftovers. Some of it was spoiled. She'd had tenants before who didn't discard food, leaving it to Diana to do so. She hated the smell that permeated the refrigerator at times, and indeed right now. Maybe she ought to buy another small fridge to replace the one that used to be upstairs? But no, then the whole house would stink.

After wrapping all the meats in Ziploc airtight bags, she put a note on the shelf to Basia:

"Please freeze these meats if you're not using them right away. Thank you."

She spread her toast with the preserves and sat down in her living room reading chair with The Sunday *New York Times.*

I must stay calm, Diana thought, *while getting used to Basia as a tenant.* Cassie purred on her lap, Juan on a pillow, and Wally on the floor nearby, snoring.

She read for about an hour, browsing the main section, all about Obama and the convention, the upcoming Republican convention, and the Book Review. Brett must have fallen asleep; it was quiet. She decided to sort her laundry in the basement. Tomorrow, she would change the sheets on her bed just in case. . . .

Oh, stop, she told herself. *You're not going to bed with the guy the first time he visits you.* But she would change the bed, anyway, *just in case.*

As she walked down the stairs, she hummed "Getting to Know You" from *The King and I.*

And there, from the steps, was a sight from a movie, a disturbing, scary movie, one she would never sit through. One-quarter of the huge basement, at least, was loaded now with Basia's belongings.

Boxes of every size; suitcases, dress bags, plastic cartons, and cardboard ones were piled up in front of her. Damned if Basia hadn't dropped all this stuff right where it blocked Diana's winter clothing, her linens, Christmas decorations, and her laundry area. *The goddamn hoarder*! Couldn't she have stored everything on the far side of the basement where there was more room? This all had to go into storage. *Immediately.*

She heard Brett's footsteps, and after attempting to sort some laundry to wash later tonight, she walked wearily up to the main floor.

"And what's the matter with you?" Brett asked. "You're not happy to see me?"

"That woman. I should never have let her move in," Diana said. "The refrigerator. The basement. The rooms upstairs. She's taken over. I'm helpless. She's an alien being, and I'm stuck with her."

Brett hugged her. "I know it's hard, especially after having Mark, the dirtbag, living here. You'll either get used to her or toss her out on her ass." He handed her Wally's leash. "C'mon, let's go to the village."

Diana took a sweater and followed him to the door.

"I'm here for another few weeks. You have me, and you have Frank. We're not going to let Basia run you over."

She attempted a smile. "That's a good way of putting it. I feel like a steamroller is heading toward me. This woman could flatten me, body and spirit."

Chapter Sixteen

It felt good to be out in the cool night air, walking with Brett again. Diana would miss him after he returned to college in mid-September.

"I'll be back," he told her now. "How can I stay away?"

"Why can't you be thirty years older, Brett? You'd be perfect for me."

"Well, at least twenty," he replied. "Older women are the thing these days."

"Even for gay guys?" Diana smiled.

"I don't think you'd make a very good fag hag."

She laughed and put her arm through his. "I met a man yesterday."

"Really? That's good to know. Tell me about him." The dogs walked ahead of them, cutting in and out of the pedestrian traffic. Sometimes Wally and Buster crossed the sidewalk, from one side to the other, causing their leashes to get tangled.

"I don't know what's to tell yet. I'll know more after tomorrow."

"You have a date." He didn't ask; he stated the fact.

Diana nodded.

"He's a good guy?"

"Seems so." She shrugged. "He's the only man in quite a while that I've been attracted to."

"What about Frank?" Brett untwisted the leashes as he spoke. "Behave, dogs!"

"You know my feelings for Frank. You're young, but you can understand, I think."

"Sure. He's a super nice man, and he's your friend. But it can't go any further, right?"

"I can't force myself to have feelings for him," Diana said. "It doesn't work that way."

"I may be young, but it happens at my age, too."

"Nothing may happen with this new guy," she told Brett. "It's only a first date. I surely don't want to hurt Frank. I'll see how things go with Tom before I tell him."

They sat on a bench on Main Street. It was a clear night. The stars and the moon were already visible. People—couples, families—passed by with ice cream from a nearby shop; others were coming and going from the movie theater. Most of the stores were still open on this Sunday night of the Labor Day weekend. Elie Tahari, J. Crew, Bookhampton, and all the others. The tourists would soon be gone; the shops would reduce their hours, and some would close their doors until next spring.

"The summer went so fast," Brett said. "Can you believe it?"

"How am I going to replace you?" Diana held his arm. "I think you should quit school and stay here."

"I've thought about it," he told her. "But I decided I should finish my degrees. That way, I'll be employable in case you flip out due to all your bad tenants and need me to support you."

She reached over to kiss his cheek. "I've been thinking that maybe I should do it: get a real job again. I'm not that old. I know of two librarian opportunities right now. I could make a good enough salary to take in maybe one tenant. If I got the right person in the house, he or she would also be good company."

Brett laughed. "Not as good as *moi*!"

"Of course not, silly, but maybe half as good."

He nodded. "Want to eat?"

"Yeah," Diana said. "I'm getting hungry."

After crossing Newtown Lane, the two of them walked to Babette's restaurant where, fortunately, there was an outside table waiting for them and the dogs. The waitress brought two plastic bowls, which she placed under the table, and a container of water.

They ate leisurely—the soup du jour made with summer vegetables, a basket of homemade bread and rolls, followed by a shared plate of fish tacos. These were made with fresh-caught Montauk striped bass, tomato, avocado, greens, and red onion, with jalapeno salsa. Sweet potato fries were served on the side.

Later, the waitress told Diana that the owner wanted them to have desserts "on the house."

"That's because we've eaten here many times before, right?" Brett looked around at the other diners.

"We're pals. She doesn't want us to go away hungry."

Warm apple crisp and a slice of strawberry-rhubarb pie, both topped with homemade vanilla ice cream, arrived, and they shared both plates.

"Thank you, Lady Babette." Brett groaned with pleasure as he ate.

"We are so lucky, right?"

He sighed. "I'll miss this," he said, eating every last bite.

"Yes, I will, too." Diana got up from her chair as he paid the bill.

They took another walk, further up Newtown Lane, to the railroad station and back again to where Brett's car was parked, south of Main Street.

Once home, they noticed that Basia's car was not in the driveway.

"Maybe she changed her mind and left to live someplace else," Diana said.

Brett let Buster off his leash. "Or maybe she was in a terrible accident and is about to die somewhere not too far away."

"Don't say that!"

He shrugged his shoulders and stepped aside so she could enter the front door. "Anything's possible."

Diana changed into her comfortable long skirt and cotton top while Brett and Buster went upstairs. He came down again within fifteen minutes after talking on the telephone. She could hear him while she was in her bedroom.

"I'm going out for a while," he said.

"Got a date?"

"I met someone at the office. He's a graphic artist and knows about architecture. We're going to meet for drinks."

"Go. Enjoy. Buster will be fine."

"Thanks, Mom." Brett put his arm around her shoulder and kissed her cheek.

She laughed. "At least you don't call me 'Grandmom.'"

"You're too young and beautiful for that."

"Flatterer." Diana waved him off. "Have fun."

She turned on the computer so she could check her email. Another message from Tom!

"I look forward to seeing you tomorrow. If I come out early enough, I'm hoping you'll drive me around and show me some of the major sights of the Hamptons."

Diana wrote back, trying not to appear too eager in her message: "I'm glad you'll be spending time out here, Tom. I hope to see you in the late afternoon so we can look at all the sights in daylight. Looking forward!"

Maybe she'd show him the sunset down at Maidstone Park or drive out through the Napeague Stretch, from Amagansett to Montauk. Then they would go down West Lake Drive to the harbor and have dinner at Gosman's, on the inlet leading to the ocean.

She would dress carefully. A navy blue top, with a bit of décolletage perhaps, and simple jewelry. White slacks and sandals. Her hair would shine in the sunlight and, later, under the restaurant's lamps—a glamorous movie actress visiting "The End," as Montauk was called. Tom would be dressed in street clothes, looking very different from the half-naked man she'd been thinking about since they'd met. Diana hoped she would find him attractive, fully dressed.

They would eat a wonderful seafood dinner: lobster or fresh-caught fish, rice or baked potato, and salad. Tom would insist that they share a dessert with their coffee or tea. They would talk for hours, long after everyone else finished their meals and left. There would be laughter as they shared their pasts, their presents, and their dreams. The sky would be glowing with stars and, maybe, moonlight.

Finally, Tom would check his watch and say that he had to leave and get back to the rez. Tomorrow, he would return to South Dakota. He hated to leave her, though. He would take hold of her hand and tell her how beautiful she was, how special, how he would not forget this evening or her. She would always be in his thoughts.

I should be writing romance novels, Diana thought. She shut down the computer and curled up once more with *The Times*. Enough of the political news. And of Hurricane Gustav, which was supposed to make landfall tomorrow morning, in Louisiana. She skimmed through Arts and Leisure and the Styles section to read the bridal notices. She liked to read about how the couples met and to read about their backgrounds. Tonight, this especially interested her.

Eventually, she slipped the movie into her DVD player and started to watch *North by Northwest*. She loved the soundtrack music and was engrossed in the scene where Cary Grant first meets up with Eva Marie Saint on the train.

Then the front door opened. Basia marched in, her tall heels bouncing along the hall floor. She wasn't alone. The son of a bitch who broke her heart was with her. Diana lowered the volume.

"*Allo*," Basia said, entering the room. She was carrying a bottle of wine. "Did you have a nice day?"

"Yes, thank you," Diana replied. "I was upstairs earlier. You did so much work in your room."

She would not mention the gross-smelling meats in the refrigerator. One complaint at each meeting was more than enough.

Nor would she mention the clothesline, which still hung outside. Diana would personally hack that down in the morning if it was still hanging there. Or maybe she would wait until Tom arrived. He could do a ceremonial dance around it before setting it on fire with one of the tiki torches she kept in the yard.

"Don't worry, Diana," Basia said. "I moved many things from the room. But I will put it all back in place when I leave someday."

Someday? Dear God.

"Maybe you and Steve can lift some of the stuff from the guest room to the basement? I want you to move all your things down there, to the far corner where there's much more space."

"Oh yes. We do that very soon." Basia looked over at Steve, who hovered in the half-darkened hallway.

Diana couldn't really see him, but she gave a half-hearted wave. Tomorrow, she would tell her to remove all her stuff and put it into a storage facility.

"Good night," Basia waved the bottle and followed Steve upstairs. Obviously, her heart had healed.

Diana rolled her eyes and turned up the volume. She thought about past tenants who brought home girlfriends or boyfriends. Hardly any of them told her beforehand, which she had believed would be a simple courtesy. When the tenants first moved in, the issue was discussed and always agreed to. Suddenly, one of them had a guest, a bedmate for the night, with the accompanying noise and annoyance of conversation and footsteps, squeaking bedsprings and moaning, extra showers, and more activity in the kitchen. A few times, the bedmate kept returning, and Diana had to remind her tenant that the room was for one person only.

If it was love or unstoppable lust, the tenant gave notice and left. Twice in one year that happened. A woman in her mid-twenties moved into one room and an older guy, in his late-thirties, into the other. They fell in love, but not with each other. Now four people instead of two were using the bathroom. They were all fine, decent people. Two were manageable; four were not.

One of the "extras," as Diana called him, even started painting some of the rooms in the house. "It's the least I can do," the fellow said with a big smile as he moved furniture, spread paint cloths, and went to work on the bathrooms, her bedroom/office, and the hallways.

Within two months, the female tenant and her boyfriend told her they were moving in together, into an apartment they had found. The other couple? The girlfriend was in the United States from Portugal on a temporary visa; Diana's tenant decided to marry her "to keep her legal." They moved out, too.

She continued to watch the movie. Hitchcock was brilliant. It didn't matter that she had seen this movie twice before; it was always fresh with surprise nuances, dialogue, or actions she hadn't noticed before. The scenes at the Plaza and Grand Central, then at the estate on Long Island, and at the U.N.—and especially on the train, with Cary Grant and Eva Marie Saint—how perfectly they all fit together and moved forward toward the climax and conclusion. Diana was tempted to push ahead and get to the South Dakota scenes, especially Mount Rushmore, but she restrained herself.

Upstairs, all was quiet for or an hour or so. When Hitchcock finally got to the part that Diana wanted, with James Mason finding out about Eva's deceit, then Cary and Eva running off to climb Mount Rushmore, long, low sounds and bouncing bedsprings could be heard from the hall and over the dining room.

"Damn," Diana said, and she turned up the volume. She was not going to miss this part of the movie; no way. Basia and her lover could screw themselves right through the ceiling. Wally, near her side, looked up at her then at the ceiling, whining.

"It's okay, boy," she said, petting him. "I wish I could have you run up there and attack them, but we'd both get into trouble. We don't want to go to jail, do we? Or to the pound?"

Diana was totally into the Mount Rushmore scene, and she followed the film to its dramatic, satisfying end, staying as focused as possible while the lovers continued their noisy coupling overhead.

Sighing, she finally turned off the film, shut down the living room lights, and walked into her bedroom, where she couldn't hear as much from up above. She took *The Times* and her cup of tea with her. Wally and the cats followed.

I'm a prisoner in my own house, she thought, clenching her fists. It had happened so many times before.

"I'm taking this too seriously," she said to Wally, as if he might understand. "It's sex. It's normal. It's what lovers do when they make up."

Diana thought again about Kenneth, her past love, from Washington. He was a good man, and he was sexy. He made *her* sexy, too.

She put the papers down on the bed and changed into her nightshirt. He had come along too soon; that was the problem. *Where was he now? Did he find someone else to love?*

She groaned, loud enough for Cassie's ears to perk up; the cat moved away from her. It would have been lovely to have had Kenneth nearby, like in her marriage, and to share the special closeness she once knew with Gary.

It would be a blessing, a real gift, if it happened now, if she fell in love again. Diana looked at her hand. She had not removed the turquoise and silver ring since Tom had placed it on her finger Saturday afternoon.

Propped up by her big feather pillows, Diana sat in bed and read. After a few shrieks and loud laughter from Basia, the commotion from her room eventually ceased. She read some of the Sunday Business Section and the Arts. Finally, her eyes kept closing. It had been a long day. She turned off the light and slid down under the covers.

RULES FOR TENANTS:

Please give me an emergency phone number.

Chapter Seventeen

At ten o'clock Monday morning, the Labor Day holiday, while Diana was in the kitchen preparing her tea and oatmeal, she heard Basia and her boyfriend saying goodbye at the front door. She watched as Steve walked to his blue van, climbed in, and left.

"Good morning," Basia said cheerfully, coming into the kitchen. She was holding her wallet. "I want to ask you—can I call my mother in Poland?"

Diana thought before replying. In a few seconds, the names of past tenants and bed and breakfast guests flashed before her. She didn't quite remember the faces. What she remembered were the telephone bills after they were gone: Ireland, $24.00; Australia, $33.00; India, $51.00. The guests didn't bother to ask if it was okay, and she couldn't find them after the bills showed up.

"I have phone card." Basia took it from her wallet and showed it to Diana. "I am having poor reception on my cell and really must call Mama."

"Sure," Diana said, forcing a smile. "Go right ahead."

After punching in all the numbers, Basia walked into the hall, taking the portable phone upstairs with her.

Diana ate her breakfast in silence, planning her day and looking through some of her mail. She had not touched the small pile since Friday. She looked at the invitations to upcoming events at Guild Hall and the Bay Street Theater. September and October meant concerts, plays, and films that would not be crowded with people like they were all during the summer.

Basia came back down and put the telephone in its cradle. "Thank you. My mother is not feeling so well. She has nerves."

"A nervous condition?"

Basia nodded. "I can't afford to go visit her, and she is afraid to fly. That is not good for her nerves. She misses me so much."

"Dear," Diana said, gently as possible, "we have to discuss a few things. . . ."

"About Steve? You want to complain about my boyfriend sleeping over?"

"Is that what you think?" Diana was startled at how quickly Basia reacted.

"You said before I moved in, no boyfriends overnight."

"Ah, you remember that."

"We had a fight. We made up. That's how it happened. I didn't plan it."

"No. No, of course, you didn't." Diana frowned. "And he won't stay here too often, right?"

"Right. We stay at his place, too. It's hard for me, this rule," Basia said, pouting. "I'm a grown woman. I like to be with my boyfriend."

Diana sighed. *So would I.*

"There are a few other matters," she said.

"I know. I know. The clothesline. I will take it down and hang my things in the branches of the trees or lay it down on the grass."

Smart-ass.

"Whatever you decide, Basia. And please ask first if you want to put anything up inside or outside the house. Okay?"

Basia did not answer; she just stared. Diana wanted to run outside right now, cut down the clothesline and strangle this pushy broad with it. Instead, she spoke softly, "We have to talk about the laundry. When I have clothing in the dryer, please wait until I remove my things, and then go ahead and dry your wash." Basia stood up straighter. "I can do that. Or, if you don't mind, I can make sure your laundry is dry, and I will fold it for you."

"That would be fine; I would appreciate it."

"No problem. I like to help. You'll see, Diana, I'm very good taking care of house."

"And one more thing, all that food you have?" She had Basia follow her into the kitchen, where she opened the refrigerator door. "That's a lot of stuff in there. You'll see that I wrapped it up for you and left a note."

"Thank you," Basia said, genuinely pleased. "I bought those meats in Riverhead last week, in Polish Town. What a wonderful butcher shop!" She picked up a few of the packets. "You can help yourself to any of this that you want. Maybe Frank would enjoy it, too."

"That's so generous of you." Diana didn't intend to eat a single bite of those repulsive-smelling meats. She wouldn't even feed it to Wally. "Do you think you can freeze some of it?" she asked.

"Oh sure," Basia said. "I do that right now." And she started moving the Ziploc packets into the freezer.

"And what about all that other food?"

"I take care of it," Basia assured her. "No problem. Anything else?"

"All that stuff you have in the basement. As I said last night, you have to organize it better. I'll be glad to help you."

"Oh no, Diana. I'll move all of it. I'm home for part of today, so I'll go down and take care of it."

She wouldn't bring up storage. Not right now. "Well, that's great. I have to go out for a couple of hours. Maybe you could let Wally out if he barks?"

"Of course. Come here, baby." Basia pulled the dog to her and kissed his head. "You let me know if you want to go pee-pee, and I will come right down."

Diana felt better; they had discussed things. "I'll see you later," she said as Basia turned to go back upstairs.

"*Ciao.*"

Diana drove to the IGA, outside of the village, and bought a few groceries: bananas, cereal, bread, tea. She drove through town, past the Hook Windmill on North Main Street, to see if the roads had fewer people and less traffic. When Jennifer and Dennis were small, she used to drive them, on Labor Day, to Cove Hollow Road and Montauk Highway, west of the village, where they would all sit in the grass and wave goodbye to the cars heading back to from wherever it was they came. Gary joined them a couple of times.

"This is ridiculous," he said more than once. "A total waste of time."

Diana enjoyed it, though, and so did the kids. All summer, they were told:

> "No, you can't take your bike here or there; too many people around." "No, we can't go to the beach; we don't have a sticker for that one" or, "It's too crowded with all the tourists."

After driving through the village streets, which were still crowded, as was Montauk Highway heading both east and west, she decided to stop at Frank's for a brief visit.

Feeling guilty? she asked herself. *With a new man on the horizon?*

"Well, look who's here!" Frank welcomed her at the door of his cottage with a bear hug. "You missed me, right?"

"I guess so," Diana said, kissing him on the cheek.

"Come on in. I'm making lunch—there's plenty for the both of us."

She settled herself at his kitchen table. The house was small and compact. There were two bedrooms, one that Frank slept in and one that he used as an office. The living room lined up next to the eat-in kitchen. It wasn't big, but it was homey and nicely decorated with Frank's refurbished yard sale and thrift shop finds. The green and brown duck decoy he had restored was still on the shelf above a cabinet, the aged print of a field and farmhouse on the wall. Frank's wife lived in town, in the marital home they jointly owned.

"I don't know if I should eat," Diana looked at the food. "I have to go out later for dinner."

"Oh, c'mon, have some. What're you drinking?"

"Just water," she said.

"You got it." He grabbed a cold bottle from the refrigerator and handed it to her.

"*Bon appetite, mon cheri.*" He took a large swig of his bottle of Diet Coke. "What a nice surprise. Happy Labor Day! Here's to Grover Cleveland."

"Why him, of all people?" She raised her glass.

"He signed the holiday into law. 1894. You don't know that?"

She smiled. "You've been at the computer."

"Of course."

One small sandwich—sliced grilled chicken breast—and she was done.

"C'mon," Frank said. "Have some more."

"No way. I could barely eat this; I may collapse from satiation."

Frank laughed. "Good word. A librarian's word. And a journalist's, too."

They talked about the conventions, the upcoming hurricane, and about a Guestwords column he was writing for *The East Hampton Star* about the dramatic change in the East End landscape; how it had changed from potato fields to a lot more houses, plus horse pastures and vineyards.

After an hour, she looked at her watch. "I've got to get home. I'm waiting for a phone call."

"Okay, okay," Frank said. "Have a good time tonight. I'll call you tomorrow afternoon."

She waved him a kiss, then left.

Chapter Eighteen

It was 2:30 when Diana arrived back home. Plenty of time to hear from Tom. As she walked down the hall, she noticed that the house had been cleaned. The carpets were newly vacuumed, the floors polished, the shelves and furniture dusted. In the kitchen, the counters, the stove, the refrigerator were immaculate inside and out. On the sofa, there was a stack of newly washed, dried, and folded laundry. She looked out the window to the yard. No more clothesline! She held her breath.

When she walked into her bedroom, she could see it was also newly dusted, vacuumed, and the bed spruced up. Her desk, too, was tidied up, folders and bills neatly stacked, with pens and pencils where they belonged, in the "I am a Librarian" mug. Basia came in *here*—into her bedroom and office, her private domain, her sanctuary?

Next, she realized that Wally was gone. Why hadn't she noticed this right away?

"Where's my dog?" she asked aloud. "What did she do with my dog?"

Cassie and Juan were missing, too. Diana's heart was beating rapidly. *Stay calm*, she told herself. *Everything will be okay. Don't panic.*

On the hall shelf, she found a small note from Basia. "Wally is with me. He told me he has never has been in a convertible. So I give him a treat!"

She opened the front closet to hang up her sweater and out jumped Cassie and Juan.

"Oh, thank God," she said, scooping up the cats and hugging them tightly. But the cats meowed and wanted to be let down. Not only down, but out the back door. They might have been in the closet for quite a while.

How long was I gone? Diana wondered. She calculated two and a half hours. Basia did all this? And why?

She walked over to the telephone. *Did Tom call?* She should have given him her cell phone number, not just the house number. *Please call*, she said silently to the phone, and remembered Dorothy Parker's classic short story, "A Telephone Call":

> "Please, God, let him call me now. Dear God, let him call me now. I won't ask anything else of You, truly I won't."

She collapsed on the living room sofa. There was a tightness in her chest, and it wasn't from eating Frank's food. Why hadn't she thought to get Tom's cell phone number? She didn't like to think of herself as over-anxious. Now she had a headache, besides the tightness in her chest, and wondered if these were symptoms of an impending heart attack; or maybe even a stroke.

It was quiet; there wasn't a sound inside the house or outside. Not so much as the central A/C, a lawn mower in the distance, or even a bird flying by. Maybe she had died and was in purgatory? Or hell? Diana knew damn well it wasn't heaven. She sat perfectly still, trying not to think of anything—not of Tom, not of Wally, and not of Basia. But she had a sudden vision of her beloved dog, excited in the convertible, leaping out at the sign of a squirrel while Basia was driving on a crowded street. Maybe Wally was dead, too.

"Goddamn." It was all she could say or even think.

Then Diana heard the car, the Beetle, and took a deep breath. If Wally was okay, if he walked through the front door with Basia and wasn't injured, she would never yell at him again. She would be the perfect dog mom forever and ever.

"We're back!"

Wally raced up to her side, his tail wagging, his tongue hanging out from thirst and excitement.

She let out a large sigh as she held him close.

"What is all this about?" Diana said, one arm sweeping the room as she petted Wally with the other.

"It is a surprise for you." Basia smiled. "I told you I was cleaning lady. You've been very good to me, Diana. I wanted to do something good for you, too."

"I don't know what to say."

"Do you like it?" Basia walked around the room. "Nothing was so dirty, but I did my best to make everything shiny and clean for you."

Diana wasn't usually speechless, but words wouldn't come. She didn't feel up to thanking the young woman, and since Basia's house cleaning was meant to be a gift, it probably wouldn't be right to scold her. She said nothing.

Finally, she asked, "Did you get any phone calls for me while I was gone?"

"Oh yes," Basia said. "I forgot to leave note. Some man. Tom?"

"You answered my phone?"

"It said 'Private Caller.' I thought maybe it was Poland."

Sitting up straighter, Diana asked, "What did you tell the man?"

Basia shrugged. "I said you were out. I had no idea when you come back."

"Did you get a phone number?"

"No. As I told you, the phone said 'Private Caller. There was no number.' He said he would be in touch with you. Had to travel. Is he your relative, Diana?"

She would remain calm. She would remain dignified. "Basia, in the future, you are not to pick up my phone under any circumstances."

"If you say so. . . ."

"And you are not to take Wally out in the daytime; it's much too hot."

"Oh, it's not so hot with the top down, and we're driving fast." Basia's smile started to fade. "I do such good things for you, and you talk to me as if I am a child!"

Diana didn't reply. She was too stunned. Tom was not coming; he was leaving for South Dakota. She had foolishly dreamed up a romance, like someone Basia's age or younger would do. And all for nothing. Zero.

Soon she would be older, and frail, and unattractive, and there would be no change. She would be sitting here in this house, petting Wally, talking to tenants, good ones along with the bad, and that would be the end of the road. It could be the end of the road right now.

"It's so bad you don't appreciate all my hard work," Basia said now. "I never do this for you again. You are not grateful, I can see."

"You have to leave, Basia. I can't take this."

"I paid rent!"

"I called my lawyer," Diana looked at her. "You have to leave." She lied, but so what? "You didn't pay me the full amount."

"I will *not* leave," Basia shouted. "You are crazy woman!" She turned around and left, slamming the front door behind her, and took off in her car.

After a few minutes, Diana got up and called Frank.

"Basia cleaned the house while I was visiting you," she told him. "And she was answering my phone calls, the nervy thing!"

"Funny, I called you earlier," Frank said. "It must have been right after you left your house. I didn't think to mention it when you were here. I think she's a lovely gal, Diana." He chuckled. "She offered to come here and massage me whenever I want."

When Frank called, the caller ID didn't say "Private Caller." Diana knew that it gave his name and number. And she didn't get Frank's message, either.

"Don't be too hard on her, Diana. You could do worse."

"I wonder. . . ."

After they spoke, she hung up and called "private caller." No reply.

Maybe Tom would call again? Maybe. And would it be from South Dakota?

RULES FOR TENANTS:

Keep front and rear doors locked when leaving.

Chapter Nineteen

Brett came home at four o'clock. He ran up the stairs with Buster but quickly came back down. "Have you seen how that Polish wretch has decorated the bathroom? She replaced your shower curtain and rugs with this frilly, beige thing. And she's got all this gold stuff—a tray with small containers of lotions and oils—on the sink counter. Not an inch of space for any of my things."

Diana sighed. "While I was out, she cleaned the entire house. Look around."

"So now you have a free cleaning service? That's a plus."

"I don't know that it's free. Basia owes me rent and security. This could be how she intends to pay me."

Brett nodded. "Her idea of bartering."

"She answered my phone while I was gone," Diana said. "Tom called. She said I was out and didn't bother taking a message. I tried to call back, but how do you reply to 'Private Caller?'"

"So, no date?"

"No nothing." Diana started to cry. "Maybe it wouldn't have led to anything, but I wanted to at least get to know him."

Brett sat down next to her and put his arm around her shoulder. "You know perfectly well it's not the end of the world. It's probably not even the end of this new relationship."

"I can't take that woman living in this house. She's just too much."

Brett stared out the back door. "I see she took down the clothesline that you hated."

"She should never have put it up." Diana stood, her tears turning to anger again. "And she shouldn't impose herself on this household by doing over her room and the bathroom, filling up the small room and the basement, telling Frank she'll come to 'massage you anytime.'" Diana mimicked Basia's voice. "When I want a cleaning woman, I hire one, damn it. And I don't let them clean my desk and all my personal things in the bedroom."

"That would freak me out, too," Brett said.

Diana stood and took a few more deep breaths. "I want so much to go up there, grab all her stuff and throw it in the driveway—clothing, linens, shoes. I know a woman who did that to her husband's things. Next, she set them on fire."

"Nice," Brett said. "Is she still in prison?"

She drew in her breath. "I can't do it, right? It's against the law."

"You could call the police and ask. But I think you know the answer."

Diana sat down again on the sofa. "It would also be too much work."

"Get rid of her then."

"Three in a row! First, a guy who stayed here during the spring. He tried to move in his 15-year-old girlfriend. Next, I had Mark. Now, it's Basia. That room is bad luck this year."

"So you change your luck. The next tenant could be perfect." Brett said. "Almost as good as me."

"I'll do it," Diana said, nodding. "Whatever it takes. I'll give her money back if I have to; anything to get her the hell out."

"Now you're talking," Brett patted her on the back.

"She has to move out and find another place."

"Like tomorrow?"

"Like right now." She walked toward the telephone. "I'll call her and tell her."

"And what if she gives you a hard time? Basia seems to know how to get under your skin."

Diana thought about this. "It's true. I don't know why, but you're right. If she stayed around for a while, I might actually get desperate enough and sell the house.'"

Her shoulders slumped, and she sat back down.

Brett spoke softly. "You love it here, Diana. I don't know that you'll ever leave. This is *your* place. You're the *landlady*. Lady-of-the-land. Get it?"

She nodded but then tears fell down her face. "I may have to live here all by myself. I can go back to work, as I told you I've been thinking about, and do without tenants."

"They're good company, a lot of them," Brett said. "You're a very giving person and, sure, certain people who move in take advantage of that."

"Even if I continue being a landlady, Brett, I'll have to accept the fact that I'll probably be a single, lonely woman for the rest of my life." She dabbed at her eyes with a tissue.

"Yes, Diana, 'even if.'"

She gestured toward the basement door. "Will you help me move some of Basia's things out to the driveway?"

"Do you mean now? Aren't you going to talk to her first?"

"We'll start moving her things right this minute, just to make sure I don't back down. I'll talk to her later."

"Okay," Brett said, "but I hope this doesn't get you in trouble."

"I don't care."

"Maybe if we just move some stuff up to the hallway rather than outside." Brett pointed. "That might cause you less legal problems."

"Hmm." Diana forced a grin. "And then I wouldn't be tempted to set her things on fire."

"Right. And I wouldn't have to visit you in jail."

The doorbell rang, and the two of them jumped.

"Did you change the locks already?" Brett asked. "She can't get in?"

Diana pushed him playfully and walked down the hall to see who was there.

It was Tom.

"I was hoping this was the right house," he said, waiving his cell phone and smiling. "Not that easy to find in these woods, even with a GPS."

What a different guy he was in regular clothes. Sharp, angular features with those dark eyes and carefully coiffed black hair. *So handsome.*

Diana knew she must look dreadful, teary-eyed, her makeup worn off, worry lines creasing her forehead.

"Well, you found it, and that's wonderful." She opened the door wide.

Tom raised his right arm, Indian style. "How!"

Diana did the same. "'How' to you, too, Tom." She stepped aside. "Come on in."

When she reached out her hand, he held on to it, smiling at Brett as he kissed her on the cheek.

"I'm her tenant." Brett shook his hand. "Pleased to meet you, Tom."

"Likewise."

The dogs circled this new man, their tails wagging.

"Wally, my dog," Diana said.

"And this is Buster." Brett picked him up and held him.

Tom nodded. "So your tenants are allowed to bring pets here, Diana. How civil you are, and what a delightful landlady you must be."

"Most of the time she is," Brett said, glancing at her.

As Diana led Tom into the living room, with him still holding her hand, Brett continued. "Right now, she has a real problem tenant to deal with."

"Really?" Tom sat down on the sofa, gesturing for Diana to join him.

She studied the sleek dark hair, the white and gray striped shirt, the dark gray slacks, and the navy sweater draped around his shoulders. Brooks Brothers all the way—from almost-naked Indian attire to this preppy look.

"We were just getting ready to toss out some of the new tenant's stuff," Brett continued. "Pile it up in the hall. You could join us if you'd like."

Diana looked up at him and then at Tom. "I don't think Tom came here to help us with that," she said.

"I might," Tom shrugged. "I'd have to hear more about it. You'll tell me, Diana?"

Brett took this as his cue to leave.

"Gotta go. Have a nice afternoon. Nice to meet you, Tom."

"Same here. Hope to meet you again."

Again.

Brett and Buster left the house. All was peaceful and quiet; no radio or TV, no distractions; Tom and she were alone, sitting on the sofa, still holding hands. Did he feel as awkward as she did? It didn't seem so.

"Can I get you some tea or coffee?"

"No thanks." He looked around. "Lovely home you have. I noticed the gardens out front and in the back: all those trees and that enormous stretch of lawn. What I'd like is for you to show me around East Hampton and the other villages. The beaches, too." He looked at his watch. "We have a few more hours of daylight."

Diana nodded. "We'll do that."

"And I want to hear about your bad tenant."

She sighed. "That could take the rest of the daylight hours, I'm afraid."

"I guess so—if you were preparing to move her belongings up into your hallway."

"I wanted to throw it in the driveway," she said, pointing. But Brett suggested the hallway." She sighed. "So I wouldn't have to deal with the police."

Tom nodded. "Is she that bad, Diana? Can't you negotiate with her, or at least try that. Sit down and make a list of what you both want and need; speak with her one-on-one before you evict her?"

"I'm so angry. She's been here less than a week, and I don't see how I can live with her on a long time basis. Evict her? That process could take a lot of time."

"You decide on a deadline, the two of you. If you don't mutually agree on the terms of her staying here, then you end the tenancy."

Tom lifted her hand to his lips and kissed it gently. "I'm a lawyer, remember? I know about real estate law. Criminal law, too. Let me hear the whole story while we're out this evening, and I'll give you my advice."

Diana reached over and kissed him on the cheek. "No charge?"

He laughed. "No charge. I'll even take you to dinner, wherever you want."

"I wish you were a New York lawyer."

"You've heard of pro hac vice? He pronounced it as "pro hack vee-chay."

"No."

"It refers to an out-of-state lawyer being admitted in a local jurisdiction for a particular case only."

"My case?"

"Correct." He looked at his watch again. "Now, let's get on the road, my lady."

"What an evening we'll have." She studied her face in the mirror, added some lipstick, and picked up her sweater and purse. "I do wish we had more time."

"We do. I canceled my flight and all my appointments this week. I'm not leaving until Saturday."

She pressed her hand tightly into the chair. "Time to get to know each other!"

Tom smiled as she said the words. "Exactly." He held her arm in his and led her to the door.

"I feel as if I'm in a film, Tom. I'm waiting for the music to start, the tom toms to beat, the dancing and chanting to begin as the credits roll down the screen."

"As they walked on together, happily ever after?"

"Something like that." She looked down at his turquoise ring.

After checking Wally's and the cats' food and water bowls, Diana locked the back door, took several deep breaths, and tried not to think of Basia or anything else unpleasant.

They embraced quickly before walking out into the cool afternoon air.

"Your car or mine?" Tom asked.

"Mine, I suppose." Diana felt chills with his hand on her arm. "I know the territory, as you Sioux would say."

"Right." Tom led her to the car. "You show me your land first, and then I'll show you mine."

Will I have to make an air reservation for Saturday? Diana wondered. *To Rapid City?* "That's so democratic of you, Tom."

More smiles, another hug, and a kiss, then Diana put the car into drive. "Off for an adventure," she said.

Tom nodded and sat back with a deep sigh, as he stared out the window.

"The first of many, my dear."

Acknowledgments

Many thanks to my fellow students in the fiction writing classes of Roger Rosenblatt and Ursula Hegi in the MFA program at Stony Brook Southampton. Their remarks, criticisms, and suggestions all helped in the shaping of this novel.

My colleagues, Elizabeth Robertson Laytin, Eve Karlin, Janet Lee Berg, Jill Evans, Rita Kushner, Marilyn Levinson, and others have been helpful with their opinions and editing of the book.

I want to thank my author friends, Tom Clavin, for help with research, and John Lindermuth for introducing me to Sunbury Press. Bill Henderson and Philip Spitzer were encouraging early on, for which I'm grateful. Andrea Meyer of the East Hampton Library kindly aided with research and Madeleine Narvilas with legal advice.

My writing students have heard me discuss *Three Rooms, Shared Bath*, and have listened to passages from the book. Over the many years of my teaching, I believe I learn more from them than they learn from me.

Much love and gratitude to my son, Jeffrey Obser, who created the map of the Hamptons inside the book.

To the Sunbury Press staff: Lawrence Knorr, publisher; Abigail Henson, editor; Crystal Devine, book designer; Ashley Shumaker, cover artist; and Joe Walters, publicist: many, many thanks for all your work. And to Harold Worwetz, my computer guy, who is always there when I need help.

With appreciation to Alfred A. Knopf, publisher, for allowing the use of quotes from *The Year of Magical Thinking* by Joan Didion.

About the Author

EILEEN OBSER holds an MFA in Creative Writing and Literature from Stony Brook University. She also has a BA in Writing and Literature from SUNY Empire State College. Eileen's articles, short stories and essays have been published in *The Philadelphia Inquirer*, *The Washington Post*, *Newsday Magazine*, *The Village Voice* and, locally, *The East Hampton Star*. Literary magazines such as *Proteus* and *The Southampton Review* have published her work, as have anthologies.

A teacher of fiction and non-fiction writing for almost 30 years at colleges, libraries and conferences, her memoir, *Only You*, was published as a second edition by Brown Posey Press in 2019.

The memoir details the first 20 years of her life, She was born and raised in Glendale, Queens, New York, attended Catholic grammar and high schools, and married a boy from her candy store crowd when she was 18, and he was 19. The year was 1960. Billy and she were two naïve, uninformed teenagers, influenced by social and religious pressures—to disastrous consequences. The marriage lasted two years.

Eileen worked for *The New York Times* Information Bureau in the early 1960s, then remarried and gave birth to two children. While a young mother she attended writing workshops at The New School and at NATAS, both in Manhattan. In 1975 she moved to East Hampton, after a divorce, and has lived there since. She has been both a tenant and a landlord during this time and is at work on a memoir about her East Hampton years.

Made in United States
North Haven, CT
22 November 2021

11392014R00104